Dear Reader,

I can hardly believe that it is almost twenty years since I wrote my first Harlequin book. The thrill of having that book accepted and then seeing it on the bookshelves—being picked up and chosen by readers—is one I shall never forget.

Twenty years seems a long time. So much has happened during those years; so much has changed and yet so much remains the same. The changes that we have all seen within society are, I believe, reflected in the books we, as Harlequin authors, write. They mirror the changes that take place around us in our own and our readers' lives. Our heroines have changed, matured, grown up, as indeed I have done myself. I cannot tell you how much pleasure it gives me to be able to write of mature—as well as young— women finding love. And, of course, love is something that has not changed. Love is still love and always will be, because love is, after all, an intrinsic, vital component of human happiness.

As I read through these books that are being reissued in this Collector's Edition, they bring back for me many happy memories of the times when I wrote them, and I hope that my readers, too, will enjoy the same nostalgia and pleasure.

I wish you all very many hours of happy reading and lives blessed with love.

Penny Jordan

Back by Popular Demand

Penny Jordan is one of the world's best loved as well as bestselling authors, and she was first published by Harlequin in 1981. The novel that launched her career was *Falcon's Prey,* and since then she has gone on to write more than one hundred books. In this special collection, Harlequin is proud to bring back a selection of these highly sought after novels. With beautiful cover art created by artist Erica Just, this is a Collector's Edition to cherish.

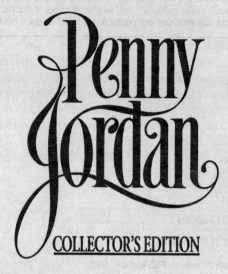

Penny Jordan

COLLECTOR'S EDITION

A Reason for Being

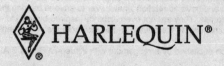

HARLEQUIN®

TORONTO • NEW YORK • LONDON
AMSTERDAM • PARIS • SYDNEY • HAMBURG
STOCKHOLM • ATHENS • TOKYO • MILAN • MADRID
PRAGUE • WARSAW • BUDAPEST • AUCKLAND

ISBN 0-373-63086-7

A REASON FOR BEING

First North American Publication 1989.

Copyright © 1989 by Penny Jordan.

ERICA JUST
cover illustrator for the
Penny Jordan Collector's Edition

Erica Just is an artist and illustrator working in various media, including watercolor, pen and ink, and textiles. Her studio is in Nottingham, England.

Her work is inspired by the natural forms, architecture and vibrant colors that she has experienced on her travels, most especially in Africa and India.

Erica has exhibited her work extensively in Great Britain and Europe and has works in private and public collections. As an illustrator she works for a number of companies and also lectures on textile design throughout the country.

CHAPTER ONE

'SO YOU'RE really going to do it.'

'I don't see that I have much choice, after a letter like that,' Maggie muttered through the biscuit she was munching.

The letter in question lay on the coffee-table where Maggie had placed it. It was written in a round, schoolgirlish hand, the letters neatly formed, much like her own handwriting at that age.

'Mm,' Lara, her flatmate, agreed, sipping the coffee Maggie had made them both. 'But girls of that age are prone to exaggeration, you know. Are you sure the situation's as dire as she says? What *does* she say, exactly?' she added curiously.

'Read it for yourself.' Maggie got up, and Lara watched thoughtfully as her flatmate walked over to the small table. Maggie never ceased to fascinate her, even now, after the length of time they had known one another. There was something very compelling about Maggie: a power she herself wasn't aware she possessed, a warmth that drew people to her. That she was beautiful as well seemed to be another unfair advantage fate had handed her. When they first met almost ten years ago, Lara had felt envious of the tall, slender redhead with her creamy skin and mysterious dark green eyes. Her envy had not lasted long. Although they were roughly the same age, Maggie had had a maturity about her, a sadness which Lara felt instinctively but had never been allowed to penetrate, Maggie being a very private person. She still possessed that slightly melancholy-tinged mystery, that aura of having withdrawn slightly from the rest of the world to a secret and inviolate place.

Maggie picked up the letter and handed it to her. Lara read it out loud, dark eyebrows lifted in faint amusement.'"Come home quickly. Something terrible has happened and we need you." Oh, come on, Maggie,' she exclaimed wryly. 'You surely aren't taking *this* seriously? If there was really something wrong, someone would have been in touch with you…a telephone call…'

'No,' Maggie told her fiercely, her expression changing from its normal one of sweetness to an unfamiliar hardness that made Lara's eyes widen slightly. She and Maggie had known one another ever since Maggie had first arrived in London and, despite her red hair, Maggie was one of the most placid and gentle people she had ever known. Which was perhaps why she had opted out of the aggressive and demanding world of art and instead used her talents to provide herself with an excellent living illustrating books.

'But surely *someone* would have got in touch with you,' Lara protested. 'Some older, more responsible member of your family.' She groped in her memory for more concise details of Maggie's family and couldn't find any. In fact, until the letters in that round, schoolgirlish hand had started arriving eight months ago, Maggie hadn't had any contact with her family at all.

She never talked about them other than to say that her parents were dead and that until their death she had lived with them in the Scottish borders where her father taught at a small private school. After their death she had gone to live with her grandfather, and Lara had rather gathered from her silence on the subject that the relationship had not been a happy one and that that was why, when she had come to London, Maggie had cut herself free of all her family ties.

And yet, from the time of the receipt of that first letter, forwarded to her by the publishers, and the others which had come after it, Maggie had changed. Not discernibly perhaps to those who didn't really know her, but the difference in her was obvious to Lara and she was intrigued by it.

What was it that lay in her friend's past that caused that unmistakable aura of restless tension to possess her when the letters arrived? What *was* it that made the swift hunger fly to her face when she opened the letters, only to be quickly controlled, as though she was desperately afraid of it being observed?

Since the arrival of the letters, Lara had realised what it was about Maggie that set her so unmistakably apart from others. It was the protective cloak of withdrawal she wore at all times to distance herself from others; she was a part of their lives at the same time as she was refusing to allow them to enter anything more than the periphery of hers. Almost as though she was *afraid* of allowing anyone to get too close to her.

A result of her parents' death, perhaps, which must have come as a traumatic shock for a sensitive child in her early teens. But Lara suspected there was more to it than that, although she was puzzled to know exactly what.

In another woman she might have ascribed the withdrawal to an unhappy love affair, but Maggie had been seventeen when she'd arrived in London, and since then the men-friends she'd had all been kept strictly at arm's length.

'I'll have to go up there,' Maggie told her, ignoring her question, her forehead pleating into a frown of concentration. 'I don't know how long I'm likely to be gone, Lara. I'll make arrangements about paying my share of the mortgage etc. while I'm gone. I'll have to get in touch with my agent...'

As she listened to her, it came to Lara that something deeply buried inside her friend was almost glad of the excuse to go home. While she talked, underneath the anxiety there was a light in her eyes that Lara had never seen before, and with startled perception she realised that she had never really *seen* Maggie herself before. It was as though the real Maggie had suddenly stepped out from behind the shadow-figure she had used as concealment.

'You know…you look like someone who's just been told they're no longer an outcast from paradise,' she told her softly.

Instantly Maggie's expression changed. Wariness crept into her face, her body tensing, as though she was waiting for a blow to fall, Lara recognised. Panic flared in her eyes, obliterating the wariness, and she said edgily, 'Don't be ridiculous.'

'*Am* I being?' Lara asked her quietly. 'We've known each other a long time, Maggie, but I think I can number on the fingers of one hand the times you've mentioned your home and family, and yet when you do…I wonder what you're doing living here in London when you would so obviously rather be with them.'

She saw Maggie go pale as though she was going to be sick, her eyes betraying her shock, but, rather to Lara's surprise, she made no protectively defensive rebuttal of her comment, saying only in a huskily tense voice, 'I *have* to go back, Lara. Susie wouldn't have written like that if they didn't need me.'

Much as she longed to ask who 'they' were, Lara held her tongue. She could see that Maggie was perilously close to the edge of her self-control— another rather odd circumstance in a woman whose smilingly calm manner was normally such a feature of her personality.

'I don't suppose you'll know how long you'll be gone?'

'No,' Maggie agreed shortly, impatiently pushing her hair off her face with one of the narrow, elegant hands that Lara, with her more stocky frame, had once envied so desperately.

'You'll have to let Gerald know you're going,' Lara reminded her.

Gerald Menzies was the latest in a long line of men who had dated Maggie. Ten years older than her, he was urbane and sophisticated—divorced, with two sons at public school and an ex-wife who was determined that, divorce or not, she was still going to live in the manner to which Gerald's wealth had accustomed her. He owned a small but extremely fashionable gallery, which was where Maggie had met him. Lara had introduced them, following an approach from Gerald to show some of her work.

Their affair, if indeed their relationship could be described as that, which Lara privately doubted, had endured for nearly ten months. They dated once or twice a week, but as far as Lara could tell Maggie felt no more for Gerald than she had done for any of the other men she had dated over the years.

No, Maggie had never been short of men willing to admire her, but as far as Lara knew she had never been deeply emotionally involved with any of them.

Indeed, at twenty-seven, they were probably the only two of their year at art school who were still not involved in a partnership of one sort or another. For Lara it was because she had ambitions that she knew were going to be hard enough to fulfil, without the added burden of a husband and potentially a family.

But for Maggie it was different. Maggie didn't share her ambitions. Maggie was made for love, for giving and sharing, but Maggie held everyone who might want to share her life at bay. Carefully, gently, almost without them being aware of it—but keep them at bay she did.

'I'll telephone him once I'm there,' she responded rather vaguely to Lara's comment.

'I've got a better idea,' Lara told her firmly. 'Why don't you telephone home and find out exactly what the problem is before you go haring up there?'

She could see that her suggestion didn't find favour with her friend, and for a moment she almost disliked herself for making it. She could see that

Maggie was struggling to find an acceptable explanation for her refusal, and, since there was something about Maggie that made you want to be kind
to her, she found herself offering, 'Or perhaps they
aren't on the phone?'

'Yes...yes. They are, but...' Maggie had her
back to her, but now she turned round. 'Yes, you're
right. I ought to ring.'

The telephone was on a small table beside the
settee. She snatched up the receiver almost as
though it was hot to the touch, Lara thought, watching her punch in the numbers with shaking fingers.
Numbers which she had quite obviously had no
trouble at all in remembering, Lara recognised on
a wave of compassion.

She touched her arm, not really surprised to discover the tension of the muscles beneath the fine
skin.

'I'll leave you to it,' she whispered, but Maggie
shook her head and grabbed hold of her, her colour
suddenly very hectic and hot.

'No...please stay.'

And, because Maggie was holding her so tightly,
she was standing right beside the receiver when the
ringing stopped and a harsh male voice said, 'Deveril House?' with a brusque impatience which, although rather off-putting, was surely no reason for
Maggie to start shaking violently. The blood
drained from her face and she slammed the receiver

back down, holding it there while she shivered and trembled and the delicate bones of her small face stood out in proud relief.

Despite all the questions clamouring in her brain, Lara managed to restrain herself from saying anything other than a dry, 'A rather formidable gentleman.'

'My stepcousin,' Maggie told her shakily. 'Marcus Landersby.'

And then she dropped down on to the settee with her head in her hands, her body racked by such deep shudders that Lara was genuinely frightened for her. Whatever else Maggie was, she was most definitely not emotionally unstable, rather the opposite, and yet here she was virtually falling to pieces in front of Lara's eyes. And the explanation for this so out-of-character behaviour lay, Lara was quite sure, with the owner of that enigmatic and grim voice.

Marcus Landersby. She tried to visualise what he might be like, but couldn't. It was like being given a jigsaw puzzle with too many of the pieces missing to form any kind of real picture.

She left Maggie and went into the kitchen, raiding their small supply of drinks to pour her a restorative brandy.

Maggie shuddered as she drank it, her eyes blank with despair when she raised her head and looked at her flatmate. 'Sorry about that,' she apologised thickly.

'That's quite a talent this stepcousin of yours has,' Lara commented lightly, watching the colour come slowly back to her skin. 'Instant and abject terror... He wouldn't happen to be related to Dracula, would he?'

Now Maggie was flushed where she had been pale.

'I can't talk about it, Lara,' she apologised huskily. 'I'm sorry... I must pack. It's a long drive home, and I'd like to get there while it's still light.'

So, for all that they had been good friends for ten years, Maggie was still not going to confide in her.

'I'm sorry,' Maggie apologised awkwardly a second time. 'It's just that...that there are some things that it's impossible to talk about, even to as good a friend as you.'

'I'll help you pack,' Lara offered, resisting the impulse to press her for at least some hint of what had happened between her and her stepcousin in the past to elicit such a reaction.

'Thanks.'

ONLY ANOTHER few miles. It was ten years since she had left here, and yet nothing had changed. Of course, she was seeing the countryside at the best time of the year: summer. In the winter these hills

were covered in snow, these small villages totally
cut off. In the winter it was quite easy to imagine
what it must have been like centuries ago, when
these border hills were the preserve of the notorious
bands of border reivers, both Scots and English,
who robbed and killed one another, often conduct-
ing vendettas that went on for generation after generation.

Her own family had been one of the most notorious of all such reivers, until they turned respectable
during the middle of the eighteenth century when
one son's marriage with a wealthy sugar heiress had
removed the need for such nefarious activities. The
need, but perhaps not the desire, Maggie acknowledged wryly. It took more than money to eradicate
that.

She was in the village now, driving past the small
church with its dark graveyard. She gave an intense
shudder of fear, remembering the starkness of the
new stone that marked her parents' grave.

With the facility she had learned over the years,
her mind switched itself off, protecting her from the
pain of memories she could not even now endure.

Turned away from her home, alone, terrified almost out of her mind by what had happened, unable
to take in how her world had fallen apart around
her, she had fled to London, desperate to lose herself and her shame in its anonymity. She shivered
despite the warmth inside her car, a moment of

blind panic attacking her. What was she doing coming back? She must be mad. She *had* to be mad…

She almost turned the car round, and then she remembered Susie's letter. 'Come home quickly…we need you.'

How could she ignore that desperate, childish plea?

Susie had been six years old when she'd left, Sara only four—the children of her uncle's marriage to Marcus's mother. Her cousins and his half-sisters.

And it had been to Marcus's care that her grandfather had consigned his underage granddaughters in his will, so Susie had told her in one of her letters.

They were a fated family, the Deverils, or so they said locally. Fated and, some said, cursed, and who could blame them for such thoughts? The death of her own parents in a car crash, followed so quickly by the deaths of Marcus's mother and her uncle, murdered in an uprising in South Africa when they were out there on holiday, seemed to be evidence that it was true.

Now there were only the three of them: herself, Susie and Sara…and of course, Marcus. But Marcus wasn't a Deveril, for all that he lived in Deveril House and administered its lands. While she… while she had been cast out of her home…like Lucifer thrown out of Heaven.

And now she was doing what she had once sworn she would never do. She was coming back. She started to tremble violently, and had to grip the steering wheel to control the shuddering tremors. So much guilt…so much remorse…so much pain. When she looked back now across the chasm of the decade which separated her present-day self from the teenager she had been, she could only feel appalled by the enormity of what she had done.

No, she couldn't blame Marcus for telling her to leave.

She was a different person now, though. A person who had learned the hard way what life was all about. A person who had learned to control those teenage impulses and emotions. Marcus would see that she had changed…that she…

Appalled, she swerved to a halt, for once uncaring of her driving, but luckily she had the road to herself. Was *that* why she was going back…to prove to *Marcus* that she had changed? No…of course it wasn't. She was going back because of Susie's letter…nothing else. What she had once felt for Marcus had died a long time ago. The shame and agony she had endured when Marcus had ripped aside the fantasy she had woven had seen to that. Not one single vestige of those teenage feelings was left. She was like a burned-out shell…a woman who outwardly possessed all the allure of her sex, but who inwardly was so scarred by what she had endured that it was impossible for her to allow herself to love any man.

That was her punishment...the price she had had to pay. And she had learned to pay it with pride and courage, unflinchingly facing the ghosts of her past whenever they rose up to taunt and mock her... whenever a new man came into her life, and she felt...nothing, nothing at all.

What she had done... What she had done lay in the past, and if Marcus tried to make her leave her home a second time she would have to remind him that, under the terms of her grandfather's will, Deveril House was one-third hers.

Although she didn't know it, the burning glow in her eyes was that of someone who had found a longed-for purpose in life. Her cousins needed her...quite why, she did not know yet, but she would find out, and, no matter how Marcus might choose to taunt or humiliate her, while they had that need she was not going to be moved from her determination to help them.

Coming back wasn't going to be easy—there would be the curious speculation of the village to face—but the long, arid years away had taught her how much her spirit craved what only this place seemed able to give her.

She had found peace here after her parents' death, and she had bonded herself to the land which had belonged for so long to her family. That she had bonded herself also to Marcus she preferred not to think about, because to travel down that path meant travelling down into the mouth of Hell itself. It struck her like a bitter taste in the mouth that, concealed within her desire to help her cousins, there might also be a kernel of her old abject and foolish need to receive absolution…to receive forgiveness…to be freed from the burdens of her past and able to walk upright once more, no longer chained by guilt and pain.

But no, that wasn't so. She had learned the hard way to come to terms with what she had done, to acknowledge that, after the way she had injured Marcus, there could be no absolution. Not from herself, and certainly not from him.

As though it was yesterday, if she closed her eyes she could still see the fury in his eyes, smell his rage like sulphur in the air, feel the shock of her pronouncement as it ricocheted around the room.

'No!' he had cried out passionately. 'God, no. None of it is true!'

And her grandfather, looking into her face, had seen for himself that she had lied. She would carry the memory of the look in his eyes with her for the rest of her life. That, and the knowledge that she had deserved every acid barb, every cruel word Marcus had thrown at her.

She leaned her head on the steering wheel, sweat dampening her upper lip, nausea clawing at her stomach, while her whole body shook with the violence of her emotions as the memories she wanted to suppress tormented her from behind the barriers she had erected against them.

But she had not wasted the last ten years, and the hardy way she fought back and regained her self-control showed the value of the lessons she had learned. Hard lessons…necessary lessons… sometimes shockingly abrasive lessons to a seventeen-year-old who, until she ran away to London, had experienced very little reality.

Guilt had motivated her in those early years, fuelling a cool independence as she fought not to give in to her need to go home.

'Get out. Get out of this house and never come back,' Marcus had said…and she had done just that, losing herself in the harsh anonymity of London's seething streets.

What might have happened to her if Lara hadn't found her? Lara, who had been toughened by her parents' divorce and the reality of travelling the world with her journalist father, living in nearly every one of its great cities. Lara, who had come across her crying her eyes out in one of London's famous parks. Lara, who had insisted on dragging her home with her. Lara, who, on learning that, like her, Maggie should have been starting art school that autumn, had prevailed upon her father to finance them both.

He was living in Mexico now, John Philips, married and retired, and they rarely saw him, but Maggie knew she would never forget him.

Financially she owed him nothing, she had paid him back every penny, and he had let her, knowing how much it meant to her; but there were other debts...and none as great as the one she owed Lara. She felt guilty that she had not confided in her friend, but right from the start she had been grimly determined that no one else should know of her folly and humiliation. Because, despite the fact that she had known what she had done was wrong, she *had* genuinely believed that Marcus loved her. She had genuinely believed that.

It was selfish, this dwelling on the mistakes of her past; she had come here for one reason and one alone. She had missed her two young cousins, the children from her uncle's second marriage to Marcus's mother, but she would never have tried to make contact with them if Susie hadn't chanced to see her name on the jacket of a book she had illustrated, and written to her care of the publisher.

They had been corresponding for eight months now. Letters she was quite sure Marcus knew nothing about.

The sickness gradually wore off and she started the engine wearily. These dauntingly draining bouts of nervous reaction had gradually lessened over the years; she had learned to recognise the symptoms

which heralded their arrival and to take evasive action. It was noticeable that she was far more vulnerable to them at such times as Christmas and family celebrations…times when the past refused to
stay locked away in the deepest recesses of her
memory.

She looked in the driving mirror and saw that her
face was reflecting her tension. She must put the
past to one side and concentrate on the present.

What would be waiting for her at Deveril House?
Why had Susie written to her so dramatically, begging her to come home? It occurred to her that it
was all too probable that her young cousin knew
nothing of the events which had caused her to
leave.

Only three people had been witness to them: herself, Marcus and her grandfather. Her grandfather
was now dead. It grieved her that she had been
unable to attend his funeral. She had only known
of his death because in those early years she had
not been able to stop herself from buying *Border
Life*, a monthly glossy based in her home county,
which had carried the news of Sir Charles Deveril's
death. It had carried something else as well, a message so stark and poignant that it was carved in her
heart.

'Maggie, please come home.'

She had ignored that message, dreading what it
portended, dreading facing Marcus…too proud and

too hurt to acknowledge even to herself how very, very much she wanted to be with him.

It had taken her years of ruthless mental self-flagellation and self-control before she had finally been able to eradicate that need, but now it *was* eradicated, she reminded herself firmly. That teen-age passion had finally died, and she had scattered the ashes so thoroughly that no embers remained to burn. Her coming back had nothing to do with the love she had once had for Marcus. It was for her cousins' sake...because of their plea...because she knew all too well the follies of which teenage girls were capable that she had come home. Home! How her own heart betrayed her, that she should still think of the weathered stone house as that.

Deveril House had been built on the spilled blood of betrayed Jacobeans, or so rumour had once had it. It was certainly true that the Deveril who had built it had heeded the advice of his cautious English father-in-law and kept himself free of any entanglement in the uprisings of forty-five, which proved so disastrous for the Stuart cause.

Whatever her ancestor's political affiliations might have been, he had been a good builder. The house stood four-square to the world, its stone walls mellowed by the seasons. Ivy clung to the east-facing side wall as though protecting it from the harsh winds that buffeted across the North Sea.

A regency rake had added an impressive

Palladian entrance before the gaming tables had claimed the rest of his fortune, and his Victorian ancestor had managed to recoup what he had lost by judiciously investing in the new boom in railways.

Two world wars had depleted the family's resources; much of the land had now been sold off, leaving just the home farm, which was tenanted, and the house and its grounds.

The property had not been entailed, and her grandfather had left the house and its land in trust for all his grandchildren.

And that included her.

Yes, she probably had more legal right to call Deveril House home than had Marcus, who only lived there by virtue of the fact that he was his two half-sisters' legal guardian and their trustee.

The future of houses like Deveril House was not a good one; even during her own short lifetime, Maggie had seen many similar houses fall into the hands of property dealers, their owners exhausted both emotionally and financially by the burden of maintaining them.

That wouldn't happen to Deveril House. At least, not during Marcus's lifetime. Her grandfather had been prudent with his money, and Marcus, whatever else his faults, would be scrupulously honest in honouring the responsibility her grandfather had placed on his shoulders.

It was whispered locally that there was a curse on the family, put there by a wild gypsy girl who had had a passionate affair with the heir to Deveril House, only to be cast off by him when his parents arranged an advantageous marriage.

Every family of long lineage in the country could probably claim similar curses, Maggie reflected wryly as her small car crested the last hill before home, and it was foolish of her to dwell too much on the many tragedies which seemed to have touched hers.

Marcus at least would be free of it, if indeed such a curse existed, since he was not a Deveril at all, and it was only by his mother's marriage to her uncle that he had been drawn into the family. There had been times when Maggie had felt that her grandfather wished that Marcus *had* been his grandson; his male heir.

It had been after hearing of her own father's death that her grandfather had had his first stroke; and no wonder, Maggie reflected, remembering her own shock and pain at losing the parents she adored.

The death of his last remaining son had exacerbated his frail condition, and after that Marcus had stood between the world and her grandfather, challenging them to disturb his fragile peace.

She had slowed down without realising it. She had the road to herself, and yes, there it was, Deveril House, viewing the surrounding countryside from the small hill on which it stood, the stone walls basking in the summer sun, as though the house wanted to soak up its warmth.

From here she could see the straight line of the drive, and the park designed by a disciple of Capability Brown and bearing all his famous hallmarks of created naturalness.

From here she could even see the swans on the small lake. Unbidden, she had a painful memory of how, when one of the farmer's sons had threatened to shoot the beautiful birds, she, not realising that he was only teasing her, had run to Marcus to beg him to intervene.

That had been in the early days after her parents' death, when Deveril, although familiar to her from her visits, was still not truly her home...when she had clung to Marcus as the only stable thing in her very unstable world, and he had patiently and kindly let her.

Marcus had been kind to her then. Too kind, perhaps, and she had turned towards him like a flower to the sun, drinking up his warmth as greedily as the stone house soaked up that of the sun.

It had surely been only natural that her adoration of him should turn to an emotional teenage crush; there was, after all, no blood tie between them. Marcus was only ten years her senior, a vital and very sensual man, who should surely have been

able to deal quite easily with the emergent feelings
of a shy young girl. So where had it all gone
wrong? How had it happened that she had become
so lost in her own fantasy world that she had actually believed Marcus returned her feelings...that
he was only waiting for her to grow up to claim
her as a woman?

She was the one at fault. *She* was the one who
had deliberately lied about their relationship, who
had deliberately tried to force... But no...even now
there were some things she just could not acknowledge; some truths she just could not accept. It was
a physical agony even now to face up to her own
failings, the muscles in her chest and throat locking
as she battled with herself, refusing to allow herself
to escape and hide from reality. From the truth.

And the truth was... The truth was that, de-
mented by jealousy, she had deliberately and wan-
tonly tried to destroy Marcus. At least, that was
what he had thought, what he had bitterly accused
her of wanting to do, and she had been too sick
with the shock of realising just where her idiotic
fantasy had led her to deny his accusations, to tell
him that it had been out of love and naïveté that
she had lied, and not out of jealous destructiveness.
That it had been because she had honestly not been
able to believe that he was getting engaged to someone else...*not* because she had wanted to destroy
that engagement... But what had been the point?

By then she had seen with appalling clarity just how foolish she had been…had realised that her dreams had been nothing but that, and in an agony of angry shame she had refused to speak a single word in her own defence, listening to Marcus's furious tirade of bitter anger as though she were doing penance. And afterwards…

And afterwards, as she stole away in the night like a thief, Marcus's words burned into her like so many brands.

Tiredly she gripped the steering wheel a little harder. Hadn't she learned years ago that there was nothing to be gained from this pointless torment of herself? She had long ago outgrown the need for self-punishment, surely…had long ago faced up to what she had done and accepted that it could never be undone.

But Marcus had never married. She had learned that from Susie's letters. Ignoring the tiny prickly feeling of sensation that ran through her, she drove down the dip and in through the open gates.

She automatically parked her car at the rear of the house, in the cobbled courtyard which had once been busy with servants and horses, or so her grandfather had told her. Now the stables were empty of everything bar Marcus's hunter, and the servants were gone. Mrs Martin, who had been her grandfather's housekeeper, had now retired and Maggie had been unable to place the Mrs Nesbitt Susie had mentioned as being Mrs Martin's replacement.

The kitchen door gave under her hand. Inside, nothing had changed, and the large, old-fashioned room was still dominated by the huge scrubbed deal table that stood in the centre. As a young girl coming to visit the house, one of the first things that had struck her about the kitchen had been its lovely smell. Her uncle's second wife had been an inspired cook, and not just that... She had grown her own herbs and vegetables, and in due season the herbs had been picked and hung up to dry in the store-rooms off the kitchen, so that their scents permeated the atmosphere.

It had been her own mother who had taught her to cook, but it had been her aunt who had shown her how to turn that basic skill into an art form.

Disappointment scored Maggie with sharp claws as she searched for the smallest trace of that once-familiar smell, but it was gone. The kitchen seemed empty and barren, not the warm, comfortable hive of activity that she remembered.

She walked from it down a narrow passage, and pushed open the door which had once marked the boundary between the servants' and the family's quarters.

The once immaculate polished parquet floor looked dusty, and Maggie frowned as the sunlight from the windows picked up the uncared-for appearance of the furniture in the sturdy square hall-way.

Six doors led off it, but she found herself walking automatically to only one of them.

Her fingers touched the cool brass of the handle. These were heavy mahogany doors, installed at the same time as the Palladian portico and owing much to the influence of Robert Adam. She knew from experience that, despite their weight, the doors would swing open without a sound, so perfectly balanced that, even after all the years which had passed since they were installed, they still opened silently.

She thought at first that the room was empty. It had the same unkempt and slightly cold air as the kitchen and the hall. This room had once been her grandfather's study, and then Marcus had made it his own private domain.

Its windows looked out on the main drive and the sweep of the park. Its marble mantelpiece was exactly the right height for a gentleman to place his glass of port on while he meditated on his business affairs; the bookshelves to either side of the fire-place were of the same rich mahogany as the door. At some stage or other, a Victorian Deveril had had the walls papered in a rich, dark green, very mas-culine silk, so that the room always seemed rather dark and overpowering.

Curtains of the same silk hung at the window,

and the Aubusson carpet had a background of the same rich green.

Either side of the fireplace stood a heavy wing chair, a huge old-fashioned desk being the only other major piece of furniture in the room, and it was only as she advanced across the carpet that Maggie realised that the chair with its back to her had an occupant, one heavily plastered leg propped up on a stool.

She knew who it was before she saw him, just by the way the hairs on her scalp prickled warningly, and it took all her considerable courage not to turn round and flee while she still could.

As she rounded the corner of the chair and came into his sight, she took a deep breath to hide her inner agitation and said calmly, 'Hello, Marcus.'

CHAPTER TWO

HE HAD changed so little physically that to look at him was to step back ten years in time.

It was true that there were small touches of grey in the black hair, hardly discernible unless one looked closely, but his eyes were the same—the pure cold grey of the North Sea—and his face still held that same quality of hard perception, that made one feel there could be no secrets safe from him.

His skin was still as tanned, his body still as physically fit, despite the encumbrances of two plaster casts, one from hip to ankle and one on his right arm. He still had that same daunting air of authority, of knowledge and intelligence, which had initially made her feel nervous of him as a teenager.

Strange, when she had met so many successful people, both male and female, that Marcus should still stand out among them; or was it simply that she was still held in thrall to her own childhood awe of him, so that she was investing him with a magical power he did not really possess?

Where she had not quailed in the presence of millionaires and politicians, she quailed a little now as that cold, searching grey gaze fastened on her, but she controlled her reaction to it, masking her thoughts from him by dropping her eyelids, so that she missed the sharp quiver of emotion that tensed his face.

There was no emotion though in his voice as he exclaimed harshly, 'My God!' He half made to start up, and then demanded instead, 'What the hell are you doing here, Maggie?'

She took a deep breath, and stepped aside from her own personal feelings and emotions as she had taught herself to do, so long ago.

'Susie wrote to me and begged me to come,' she told him quietly.

She saw his expression darken with quick, growing anger, his muscles tensing as he fought to control it.

So something had changed, after all. How many times in the past had she been infuriated, baffled and, yes, frustrated by Marcus's ability to hide his feelings from her? She had always been aware of his strength of will, or course, but, apart from the night she had run away, she had never seen him so quickly aroused to betraying what he felt.

Quite a unique distinction, she reflected grimly: to be one of the very few people he disliked strongly enough to betray an emotional reaction to.

That was another thing which had always infuriated her about Marcus: the fact that he always seemed to distance himself from others…to set himself apart and sort of look on in almost contemptuous amusement at the follies of the rest of the human race.

She had seen and met people in London who displayed the same skill, although with nothing like Marcus's finesse. They, she had learned, used it as a protective shield against the world and the hurts it could inflict; she had even learned to adopt a little of that camouflage for herself, and now, unexpectedly, beneath her firmly controlled apprehension, ran a fine thread of speculation. What was it in Marcus's life that had made him decide he needed the benefit of such camouflage?

As she observed his angry reception to her arrival, she was aware that, perhaps for the first time, she and Marcus were meeting on the same level. The ten-year gap which as a teenager had made her feel so awestruck and tongue-tied in his presence, especially when she started to suffer from that crippling crush on him, was now of no importance at all.

Yes, the disadvantage she had suffered because of their age difference had gone, but the hostility remained. And small wonder that he should resent her. He had never married—because of what she had done? It was an uncomfortable thought, and one which awoke old guilts.

'How long have you been in contact with Susie?'

he asked her harshly, trying to swing round in his
chair so that he could face her properly.

It gave her a tiny, savage thrill of satisfaction to
realise that for once he was the one at a disadvantage, both from the surprise of her arrival, and from
the fact that his heavy plaster cast made it virtually
impossible for him to stand up, so that she was in
the enviable position of looking down on him. It
was a strange sensation when she was more used
to him towering above her.

She was a fairly tall girl, somewhere around five
foot seven or eight, but she had always found
Marcus's powerful six foot two male frame a little
intimidating.

Probably because vulnerable teenage girls were,
by their very natures, inclined to be over-impressed
by such physically masculine attractions as those
Marcus possessed, she reflected cynically.

He wasn't perhaps a strictly handsome man, but
he had something more compelling than intense
good looks. He had a magnetism...a maleness that
no woman could fail to be aware of.

By the time she had come to live at Deveril
House he had been over his teenage years of dating
a different girl every month, and for a long time
there had been no serious girlfriend in his life, but
it had still been very obvious even to her that the
half-dozen or so girls who almost continuously
called round on some pretext or other whenever he

was at home were the ones doing the running in whatever relationship he had with them.

He had told her once that he didn't intend to marry until he found someone he knew he wanted to spend the rest of his life with; she, at fifteen and already desperately in love with him, had breathed safely again. If he hadn't found that women yet, then there was time for her to grow up and convince him that she was that woman.

After that she had prayed fervently every night that he would not find someone until she *had* grown up.

Her birthday fell in July, and the year before she left school, she thought that moment had actually come and that Marcus no longer saw her as a child, but as a woman.

Marcus and her grandfather between them had arranged a party to celebrate her attaining her seventeenth birthday. Her grandfather had given her some small items of jewellery which had once been her mother's: a string of pearls, the diamond pendant which had marked her own birth, and various other gifts from her father to her mother, some of which had been in the Deveril family for very many years.

As the second son, her father had always known that eventually the small estate and the house would pass to his elder brother, but that had never worried him. He enjoyed teaching, loved his quiet, calm way of life and his small family, and his father, being a wise and caring parent, had made sure that there was no rivalry between his two sons by allowing both of them to give their wives gifts of jewellery from the small number of pieces that still belonged to the family.

Maggie had also received a charmingly delicate Victorian bow brooch in diamonds and pearls for her birthday, and she had left both that and the diamond ear-rings Marcus had given her behind her when she had left. When she had realised that, far from loving her, in reality Marcus thought of her as nothing more than a difficult child...a child whom he now hated and loathed. When, as the angry lash of his acid words had flayed her tender nerves raw, she had realised that she could no longer live under the same roof as him.

He had looked at her once after he had finished castigating her, and had demanded bitterly, 'Why? Just tell me why?'

And she had turned her head in stubborn silence, too shocked and numb with the reality of what she had unleashed to defend herself.

'You'd better go,' he had told her quietly. 'Before I do something I'll only regret.'

And then, as she walked towards the door, sick with shame, trembling with the shock of his angry words, he had added rawly, 'You just don't care, do you? You just don't give a damn...'

She had managed to speak then, fighting back the nervous tremors that racked her to say huskily, 'Would it make any difference if I did?'

He had looked at her for a long, long time before saying stonily, 'No... I don't think it would. I wish you'd never come into my life. Do you realise that, I wonder? Do you realise how much I wish I never had to set eyes on you again?' he had added viciously, and she had taken those words to bed with her and had known, as she lay there sleepless and cold with shock and reaction, that there was only one course open to her.

One of them must leave, and it couldn't be Marcus. Her grandfather needed him too much, and so it must be her...

She came out of the past with a start.

Deveril House was in reality more her home than it was Marcus's, but right from the first moment she had come to live here, after her parents' death, she had associated the house with him, and therefore she had always felt that he had more claim on it than she had herself.

It was because of that conviction that she had not allowed herself to grieve over it...to miss it. Because of Marcus, she had striven so hard to remain independent of it.

Surely she had achieved that, if nothing else? she reflected with grim satisfaction, refusing to remember her seventeenth birthday party or the kiss that

Marcus had given her then...her first truly adult kiss, or so she had thought it at the time. A tame thing perhaps, by modern standards... If she closed her eyes, though, even now she could call back the rough/smooth sensation of his mouth on hers, the tension that had gripped her for that heart-stopping second of time when the pressure of his mouth had changed and she had known, gloriously and triumphantly, that he wanted her.

So much for the folly of youth.

'I *said*, how long have you been in contact with Susie?'

She took refuge in feminine vagueness, shrugging her shoulders and saying carelessly, 'I don't really know. Does it matter? Quite some time. Long enough for her to feel that she can trust me, obviously,' she pointed out with delicate unkindness, watching the colour touch his cheekbones as her thrust went home.

'Where is she, by the way?' she asked idly, as though unaware of his anger.

'She's out with a friend,' he told her grimly. 'What exactly was it she told you that made you come rushing back here, Maggie? Quite a miracle for her to perform. I seem to remember that, when your grandfather died, I put notices in every newspaper and magazine I could find, begging you to return.'

'That was different,' Maggie defended herself

huskily. 'Gramps was gone. There was no point,' she added, unwittingly betraying the fact that she had read his pleas for her to come home. 'There was nothing I could do…but this is different.' *I'm* different, she wanted to add, but the words remained unsaid. To utter them was to court danger, since he might reasonably demand to know in what way she had changed, and she would be forced to admit that it was only now, after ten years, that she felt confident enough of her self-control to be able to return to the scene of her agony.

'So…you still haven't answered my question. What did Susie tell you to bring you rushing back here?'

'I think that's between me and Susie, don't you?' Maggie taunted him, adding, 'Where's Mrs Nesbitt, by the way?'

Before he could reply, the door burst open and a stunning brunette burst in. Older than Maggie herself, she had the polished perfection which Maggie automatically associated with someone very much in the public eye and very much aware of herself and her attractions.

It was idiotic to take such an instant and strong dislike to the other woman. Maggie normally liked other members of her own sex, enjoying their company and their conversation, but this woman…perhaps it was something to do with the very hostile way in which *she* was regarding her, she reflected as the brunette demanded, 'How is my poor fiancé today, and, Marcus darling, who does that car outside belong to? Don't tell me you've actually found someone to take Mrs Nesbitt's place? I only hope this one lasts a little longer than the last replacement. You'll really have to learn to control that temper of yours if...'

'Sorry, Isobel. Not a housekeeper, I'm afraid.'

'Oh.' She turned in Maggie's direction and studied her coolly, her hand resting on Marcus's shoulder as she stood beside him.

'Then who...?' She paused delicately, eyebrows slightly raised, glossed mouth faintly pursed.

'My stepcousin, Maggie Deveril. I presume it *is* still Deveril?' he asked Maggie in an unexpectedly harsh tone.

His question caught her off guard, shocking her. Did he really think she would have married after what... Abruptly she caught herself up just in time, sensing the traitorous ground lurking beneath her feet. Of course, it was only natural that he might think her married...just as it was equally natural that he should be engaged.

Engaged... She told herself that the sick feeling gripping her insides owed its existence to the past and not the present.

'Ah, yes, I think I remember you,' Isobel commented thoughtfully, her eyes narrowing. 'You left the area rather unexpectedly, didn't you? You know, darling, you've never told me all about that. I do think family skeletons are so exciting, don't you?' she asked Maggie, focusing on her again, and then adding with a light laugh, 'Although when a young unmarried girl leaves home unexpectedly, there is normally only *one* conclusion one comes to, isn't there?'

There was a tense pause, and then her own cold, 'Is there?' and Marcus's hard, 'Isobel, that's enough,' both came at the same time.

'Teenage girls leave home for a wide variety of reasons which have nothing to do with your un-warranted implication,' Marcus continued. 'In Maggie's case it was because…'

'…I wanted to go to art school in London, whereas my grandfather would…have preferred me to attend college in York,' Maggie lied, quietly intervening.

She had no idea what Marcus had intended to say, but, if he wished to reveal her sins in full to his fiancée, then he could do so without her looking on.

'Is there no one at all in charge of the house at the moment?' she challenged him, changing the subject.

'Not as such, no,' he responded curtly.

'Poor darling. It's the pain that's making you so irritable, isn't it?' Isobel cooed sickeningly. 'Never

mind. Daddy says you'll probably be able to have
the plaster off in another six to eight weeks.'

Marcus made a sound that sounded more like a
growl of irritation than anything else, and Maggie
was hard pressed not to smile a little. How very
vulnerable he seemed now, with both his hair and
his temper ruffled, and relief flooded through her,
releasing her inner tension. There was nothing she
had to be afraid of. Marcus was engaged to be married, and she was not a child any longer, living in
a world of fantasy and make-believe. The shadows
which had dogged her footsteps for so long short-
ened a little, suddenly far less menacing.

'And what the hell do you think is so funny?'
Marcus challenged her, bringing home to her the
fact that he was far from being a helpless child.

She might not like his fiancée, but she certainly
didn't envy Isobel the task of soothing him, she
reflected wryly, as she told him sweetly, 'What happened, Marcus? Did you fall off that high horse of
yours?'

The anger that arced between them shut out Isobel completely, and for a second the present
dropped away and she was conscious of him with
all her senses, both awed and intimidated by him,
held in thrall to her childish dreams; then Isobel
said something and the spell was broken, freeing
her from its cruel bond.

She stepped back from him, feeling a need to put

an actual physical distance between them, shivering a little as she did so, and Isobel, seeing it, remarked with mock solicitude, 'Oh, dear, Marcus, Maggie is cold. Of course, you've been living in London. I do envy you.' She pulled a pretty face. 'I do manage to get down for the odd break, and I have chums down there from school and we all meet up pretty regularly, but since Daddy insisted on my helping out by acting as his receptionist at the surgery...I simply haven't had the chance. And Marcus, of course...hates me being away, don't you, darling? I take it this is just a fleeting visit?' she added with apparent casualness, but Maggie wasn't deceived. She could see how little the other woman relished her presence.

'I don't know yet,' she told her calmly. 'It all depends.'

'On what?' Marcus demanded bluntly.

Later she would have time to investigate more thoroughly that dull little pain which attacked her at his obvious desire to be rid of her; for now she had to marshal all her resources in order to be able to tell him calmly, 'On why Susie felt it necessary to write and ask for my help.'

'Susie wrote to you...' It was Isobel who responded to her, her expression changing to one of anger. 'Oh, really, Marcus, that child is getting too much,' she told him furiously. 'I keep telling you. Both of them should be at boarding-school. You

must see how good it would be for them, darling,'
she added in a more wheedling tone as she saw his
frown. 'And for us. When we get married. And anyway, now that Mrs Nesbitt's gone, what alternative
do you have, especially when you're immobilised
like this? I mean, it's all very well relying on
friends to take the girls to and from school... You
know I'd be pleased to help out myself, but Daddy
needs me too much, and frankly, darling, the girls
are getting the teeniest bit spoiled. I promise you a
few years at school will do them oodles of
good...and it will give us the privacy we both need.
Such a shame we can't bring the wedding forward
from next June, but you know that Mummy has set
her heart on a June wedding, and, as I said, Daddy
needs me to help out at the surgery...'

And wasn't she just thrilled about that, since it
meant that she was released from having to do anything about the girls, other than insist that they went
to boarding-school? Maggie reflected wryly. She
had met many women like Isobel in London: selfish, self-absorbed, completely insensitive women
who projected an image of frail femininity while in
reality being as hard as the diamonds of which they
were often so very fond.

'You can't possibly manage with them at home,
anyway. You know that it's going to be at least
another three months before you're properly back

on your feet.' She gave a small trill of laughter. 'I feel so guilty about the whole thing.'

'You can hardly be held responsible for a bolting horse,' Marcus interrupted her grimly, and Maggie, who knew quite well that Marcus rode superbly, wondered what on earth had happened to cause him to be thrown, and so violently that he had apparently broken both his shoulder and his leg.

'Well, it's just like you to be so sweet about it, but I'm terribly conscious of how many problems being immobile is causing you. What about the business?'

'My partner's taking over for the time being. I can keep up with most of the paperwork from here. My secretary has agreed to come out three afternoons a week, so that we can keep on top of it.'

'What a treasure she is,' Isobel cooed, but Marcus could see the betraying narrowing of the hard blue eyes. 'But if I could give you a little word of warning, darling. Her husband's away so much, and I suspect she's a little in love with you. It wouldn't do to let her get the wrong idea. Look at the problems it caused you before...' She gave Maggie an acidly sweet smile, and added, unforgivably, 'I'm sure, now that Maggie herself is an adult, she won't mind my saying how worried you were at the time. I mean, girls of that age don't always realise what they're doing, do they? And they can be so very, very determined. I mean, we're always reading about schoolmasters whose lives have been ruined because of the importunings of some oversexed little schoolgirl...'

'Isobel,' Marcus warned harshly, interrupting her, but Maggie had no need of his interruption. After all, Isobel wasn't saying anything about her that she hadn't already said herself; and she had long ago become inured to the pain of knowing how stupidly she had behaved. While it wasn't true that she had actually physically opportuned Marcus, she had certainly done everything she could to make him aware of her sexually, albeit within the limits of her very scanty knowledge and even more scanty experience.

'Oh, it's all right, Marcus,' Maggie told him coolly. 'I quite agree with Isobel. Teenage girls can be terrifyingly dangerous when they develop an intense crush on someone. Luckily most of us grow out of that phase,' she added pointedly, and then watched the hard colour burn in Isobel's face. 'Obviously you two must want to be on your own,' she added thoughtfully. 'I'll go upstairs and unpack. I take it my old room *is* still empty?'

She saw from the look on Marcus's face that he hadn't anticipated her question, and moreover that he was shocked by her decision to stay. Well, let him be. Everything she had just heard in this room confirmed her feeling that Susie would never have written so desperately to her if she had not genuinely felt she needed help.

At Isobel's mention of a boarding-school, warning signs ten feet high had sprung up in Maggie's brain. In the old days, the housekeeper had kept a motherly eye on Susie and Sara, and Marcus himself had taken on the role of parenting them. A deep bond had always existed between the two little girls.

Maggie had had the opportunity to get to know Ruth, Marcus's mother, very well, after her own parents died. She had married very young for the first time, and Marcus had been born when she was just eighteen.

By all accounts she had been very much in love with her older husband, a major in the army. He had been killed in action when Marcus was ten and, after all those years of being alone with his mother, it must have been very difficult for him to adjust when she eventually married again, especially when the two girls were born. He had been an adult when Susie arrived; there was a twenty-one-year gap between them, and Maggie wondered if he had ever felt any resentment. If so, she had never seen any evidence of it.

In those early days of her uncle's second marriage, she and her parents had only been infrequent visitors at Deveril House, and Marcus himself had been away at university. It was only when her par-

ents died that she had come to be more familiar
with her uncle and his family, and certainly in those
days she had discerned no resentment of his two
half-sisters in Marcus's manner towards them;
rather, he had been very much the indulgent older
brother. As he had been to her…only *their* relationship had been very different. She had clung to
Marcus after she had overcome the shock of her
parents' death, seeing him as someone she could
rely on…someone who wouldn't abandon her…
someone who cared for her. If only things had
stayed that way. If only she had continued to look
upon him as an older brother-cum-father instead of
as a man.

It made her uncomfortable even now to think of
the adolescent fantasies she had woven around him,
fantasies she had pushed to the back of her mind
until Isobel's catty tongue had recalled them.

Fantasies which had eventually led to the de-
struction of her whole world. Fantasies which had
caused scars she bore even now. Fantasies which
had caused her such pain…such guilt…and not just
her. Marcus, too, had suffered. She could never allow herself to forget that. She wondered if Isobel
knew that he had been engaged before…that he had
contemplated marrying someone else. She realised
with a slight sense of shock that she hadn't even
known the name of her rival…hadn't even allowed
Marcus to tell them exactly who it was he was get-

ting engaged to; she had been too shocked, too hurt
to do any more than protest that he couldn't, he
mustn't mean what he was saying—not when he
loved *her*!

CHAPTER THREE

THE bedroom, originally chosen for Maggie by Marcus's mother when she was first orphaned, was on the first floor of the house and overlooked the rear of the property.

As Maggie pushed open the door and stood motionlessly on the threshold, she realised with a pang of nostalgia how much she had always missed this room, and how much thought and care must have gone into preparing it for her.

Her emotions dulled by the sharp grief of losing her parents, she had barely noticed the soft sheen on the antique four-poster bed, nor the expensive luxury of its prettily faded curtains, their chinoiserie design very much in keeping with the early nineteenth-century bed.

Now a film of dust covered the polished boards of the floor and the antique dresser, but simply by closing her eyes Maggie could recall with vivid clarity the day she had first seen this room, realising now how much of its ambience her senses must have recorded and retained even though she herself had not been aware of it.

Now, coming back, she could only humbly marvel at the time and effort Marcus's mother must have put into preparing this room for her. Then the furniture had shone with polish, its scent permeating the room, mingling with the elusive delicacy of the pot-pourri mixture which perfumed every room in the house. Then the curtains had been crisply fresh on both the bed and the pretty dressing-table beneath the window.

Her aunt had helped her unpack, talking calmly and gently to her as she did so, her fingers deft where Maggie's own were clumsy. She had shown her which bathroom she was to use, half-way down the corridor, and then she had quietly and tactfully left Maggie alone in her new surroundings, whisking herself out of the door.

A huge sense of loss engulfed Maggie as she stood there caught up in the time-warp of the past, as she grieved for the grace and kindness of her long-dead aunt. She had known her for such a short spell of time and, while loving her, had not truly appreciated all that she was...had taken for granted the comfort and kindness which she had created within the old house. And now suddenly she was aware that all that was gone; that her daughters and her son had been cruelly deprived of her cherishing warmth.

Maggie crossed the faded carpet and stared out of the window, noticing dimly the faint blurring of the landscape as her emotions caused tears to fill her eyes.

She had not expected to feel like this, but now that she did she was filled with an even firmer resolve to find out what was bothering Susie and, if she could, to put matters to rights.

She strongly suspected she would learn that it was the threat of being sent away to boarding-school that was distressing her young cousins, and she could only sympathise with them.

She put her weekend case on the bed and opened it, and then turned to unlock the old-fashioned wardrobe doors. To her shock, the wardrobe still held her old clothes, and the sight of them hanging there caused a frisson of sensation to run down her spine.

The dress she had worn for her seventeenth-birthday party swung gently in its plastic cover. She reached out and touched it tentatively, and then the past and its ghosts vanished as she was suddenly struck by an idea to complete an illustration she had been commissioned to do, and she reached eagerly into her case to extract the sketch-book she took everywhere with her.

Within minutes she was so deeply immersed in her work that she was oblivious to everything else, even the opening of her bedroom door.

'So you're still up here. What...?'

Maggie's pencil snapped as Marcus's voice

broke her concentration and threw her shockingly into a pose of frozen tension. She hadn't expected him to invade her privacy like this, but rather to keep his distance, and it worried her that she should feel so disturbed by his presence.

It was because of the memories he evoked, that was all; memories of those times when she had welcomed his presence here with her.

In her frozen state of shock, it seemed almost possible that if she turned her head and looked at the bed she might see the ghost of her childhood self, sitting there cross-legged and straight-backed in the shadow of its hangings, begging Marcus to stay just a little longer, the whiteness of her cotton cambric nightdress a pale blur as she pleaded with him to stay just until she had gone to sleep.

That had been in the early days of her coming here...when her nights had been tormented by the nightmares which only Marcus seemed to have the power to hold at bay.

How often had he sat in the armchair beneath the window in response to her pleadings, reassuring her, soothing her...allowing a bond to form between them which surely in his maturity he must have realised would one day hold the elements of disaster?

'What the devil are you doing?' Marcus demanded, the abrasively harsh tones banishing her ghosts from the past and bringing her back to reality. She and Marcus might once have been close, but those days were gone, destroyed by...destroyed by her own folly, her stupidity, her lies...her love.

'Earning my living,' she told him crisply, tucking her hand beneath the pad so that he wouldn't see its betraying shake.

She saw the surprise leap into his eyes before he shuttered his expression from her, and had a moment's savage satisfaction that for once she had caught him off guard.

'You're an artist?'

She remembered how he had encouraged her interest in art in those early days, and wondered bitterly if he had known even then that she did not have the ability which would make her work outstandingly significant. Very possibly, if the look of surprise was anything to go by, and her earlier euphoria vanished, leaving her feeling drained and tense.

'Of sorts,' she told him calmly, determined not to let him see how much his comment had hurt. She had come to accept years ago that her skill would never be more than merely a very good second-rate; that was partly why she had chosen illustrating as her career. 'I'm an illustrator, and I work with a variety of writers.'

She toyed with the idea of telling him that that was how Susie had found her, and then cautiously decided against it.

'Why have you never come home?'

The abrupt question made her freeze with shock. He knew the answer to that as well as she did herself.

'Perhaps because there's never been any need until now,' she told him as lightly as she could. 'The *girls'* need, by the way, and not mine,' she added pointedly, putting down her pad and standing up. 'When will they be back?'

'Soon. Tell me something…is Susie expecting you?'

'She asked for my help,' Maggie told him evasively.

'And on the strength of that you dropped everything and came haring up here?' He looked quite deliberately at her left hand and then said softly, 'And what about the current man in your life? Doesn't he…?'

'There is no man!' she cried out, interrupting him, her face flushed and hot, her eyes bright with pain. 'Do you really think that after…'

She saw the way he was looked at her and stopped abruptly, painfully aware of how much she had been about to give away, and said shakily instead, 'And even if there were, I'm a free agent and perfectly entitled to make my own arrangements.'

'And that's the way you like it, is it? Your freedom means more to you than commitment? You prefer having a lover to a husband?'

He was looking at her ringless finger, and a wave of hot, corrosive bitterness swept through her.

'Just because you're about to get married, Marcus, it doesn't necessarily mean that the rest of the world must follow suit. I haven't congratulated you yet, by the way,' she added, turning away from him and picking up her pencils, desperately striving for the right note of casual indifference. 'I'm sure you'll be very happy together. Next June, you're getting married? It's a pity you can't bring the date forward, or am I right in thinking that Isobel would still insist on sending the girls to boarding-school? I take it the pair of you do intend to live here.'

She turned to look at him then and told herself that she was pleased to see the look of grim anger darkening his eyes. He didn't like her questioning him about his plans. Well, she was an adult herself now, and as fully entitled to question him as he was her.

'Why?' he asked her shortly.

She shrugged delicately, chewing on her bottom lip before giving him an acid smile.

'Well, this house was left to the three of us, Susie, Sara and myself, by our grandfather, wasn't it?' she asked, deliberately stressing the possessive 'our' which openly excluded him for that relationship.

'Are you trying to accusing me of stealing your inheritance, by any chance?' he demanded bitingly, taking her off guard by the directness of his question. The light slanting in through the window seemed to emphasise the hard, jutting angle of his cheekbones, lending his features a dangerous male cruelty. She badly wished she had never introduced such a dangerous subject, but it was too late to back down now.

'Hardly that,' she told him quietly, 'but this *is* the girls' home.'

'And yours?' he questioned, and an unwelcome hard lump rose in her throat at the words, because what he said was no longer true. This wasn't her home. She reached out blindly and curled her fingers round the polished wood of one of the bedposts. It felt reassuringly warm and soothing, making her aware of how cold her hands were. A sure warning of increasing tension, if she actually needed one. She had known from the moment Marcus walked into her room that her frail stock of resilience would all too easily be drained by his presence.

'No,' she told him sombrely, without looking at him. 'Not my home…' And then she looked up at him and surprised such a look of pain in his eyes that for a moment she was blinded by it, held in thrall to it and unable to drag her gaze away.

'Maggie, for heaven's sake,' he said harshly, crossing the room and circling her arm with his good hand.

Through the silk of her blouse she could feel the rough calluses on his fingers. Calluses caused by hard outdoor work, by riding…by the life he lived. His touch was so overwhelmingly familiar that for a moment she thought she was going to faint with the intensity of emotion it aroused inside her.

'Let me go,' she demanded thickly, gritting her teeth to stop them chattering together as she fought to suppress the welling sensation of aching delight wrought by his touch.

He released her as though her skin was fire, stepping back from her awkwardly, hard spots of dark colour burning his cheekbones.

'Once you wouldn't have said that,' he taunted her angrily.

Before she could gather her resources to defend herself, a car drew up outside. Marcus limped over to the window and said over his shoulder, 'It's the girls.'

'I'd like to have the opportunity to talk to Susie on my own,' she told him shakily, thankful that he had his back to her and could not see the effect he had had on her.

'I'm their guardian, not their gaoler, but remember one thing, Maggie, they're in my care. Not yours.'

Was he warning her that he wasn't going to allow her to interfere in his decisions? Well, he had that right. She couldn't deny it, but apart from that one occasion he had never been an unkind man, and she could not honestly think he would want his half-sisters to be unhappy. Manlike, he had probably allowed Isobel to convince him that boarding-school was the best solution because it removed the problem of their care from his shoulders.

Maggie gave a faint sigh as he moved over to the door and held it open for her. It was pointless making any assumptions until she had had the op-portunity to talk properly to Susie.

'AND SO YOU SEE, we can't possibly go to boarding-school. It would be horrid there, and Sara couldn't do her riding, and...'

Maggie held up her hand to stem the hot tide of protests and jumbled explanations which had been falling from her young cousin's lips for the last half-hour.

Susie had recovered from the shock of discov-ering that Maggie had responded in person to her plea with an aplomb that Maggie could only envy. It was plain to her that neither Susie nor Sara stood in the slightest fear of Marcus, because it seemed to have occurred to neither of them that he might punish them for contacting her behind his back, nor that he might resent her interference.

After a snatched high tea which Maggie had pre-pared herself from the very limited provisions she had found in the cupboards, she and Susie had retired to the old school-room on the second floor so that they could have their talk.

'So what are you trying to tell me?' she asked gently now. 'That you don't want to go to boarding-school?'

'Well, would you?' Susie asked indignantly. 'And besides, it isn't fair. Just because Isobel doesn't want to be bothered with us... I wish she and Marcus had never got engaged. I hate her. She just wants to get us out of the way so that she can be on her own with him.'

Maggie looked at her thoughtfully and then said quietly, 'People in love often feel like that.'

Susie scowled and kicked the leg of the battered chair. The school-room had originally been furnished over forty years ago, and its furniture bore the scars of the generations of young Deverils who had inhabited it.

Her own father had carved his initials inside one of the heavy wooden desk-lids, and when she had wanted to do the same thing, after he had died, Marcus had gently suggested instead that she make up a scrap-book of anecdotes and photographs of the generations of young Deverils who had worked in the room.

The task, at first a chore, had quickly become an absorbing hobby. Her grandfather had supplied the photographs, and the original book had soon expanded to include sketches and notes of things she had discovered and been fascinated by. Her glance roamed the packed bookshelves and stopped automatically at the spot where the book had been kept.

Her heart gave a tiny leap as she realised it was still there, and Susie, conscious of her lack of attention, followed her gaze and then said knowingly, 'You made that book, didn't you? Marcus told us about it. He used to be such fun,' she added with another scowl. 'But he isn't any more, and it's all because of Isobel.'

'Now that he's engaged, I expect he has other things on his mind.'

'They don't sleep together, you know,' Susie told her, shocking her with her forthrightness. 'At least, not here. I supposed it's because Marcus doesn't want to set us a bad example.' She pulled a face, and Maggie had to remind herself that at sixteen Susie could hardly be ignorant of the realities of life. 'I don't think he loves Isobel at all. He never touches her or anything.'

'Susie, I don't think you should be telling me any of this,' Maggie protested weakly, trying to deny the sensations burgeoning inside her at the thought of Marcus making love to Isobel…at the thought of him touching her…running his fingers through her dark hair and then spreading it on his pillow while he buried his face in it and… She swallowed hard, forcefully dismissing the teenage fantasies with which she had tormented herself as a young girl.

Once she had dreamed of Marcus making love to her in just such a way…had dreamed of it, and ached for it, until she had almost been able to feel the solid weight of him pressing her down against the mattress of her virginal bed.

'Why not, when it's true?' Susie protested, showing signs of the stubbornness she was cursed with possessing herself, Maggie recognised on a wave of sympathy for the younger girl.

'It may not be so bad,' she told her.

'Yes, it will. Isobel hates us. She can't wait to get rid of us. I heard her telling her mother that there was no way she was going to put up with having us hanging around.' She scowled again. 'Anyway, I think Marcus is only marrying her because he thinks we need a woman's influence…'

'Well, that's what I heard Mrs Simmonds—she's the vicar's wife, you know—saying to him. She said she thought it was time we had a woman's influence in our lives and that we were growing up very quickly, and then less than a month later Marcus and Isobel got engaged.'

'I'm sure that was just a coincidence, Susie,' Maggie told her firmly.

'Well, I don't think so. If Marcus really wanted to get married, why should he wait until now? He's pretty old, you know,' she told her with all a teenager's scorn for anyone over the age of eighteen.

He's thirty-seven, and he's never been engaged before...'

'Yes, he was...a long time ago,' Maggie said painfully, forcing herself to make the admission as she saw in Susie's eyes the younger girl's determination to do all she could to break the engagement. She could not allow it to happen...could not allow Marcus to suffer a second time, and it came to her as she looked down into the pretty, flushed face of her cousin that here, perhaps, was the means of her salvation...her way to make reparation and in so doing to free herself from the past for ever.

'When?' Susie asked her, immediately diverted. 'Was it when you lived here? What happened?'

'I...it's all a long time ago,' Maggie told her feebly, wishing she had never made the betraying comment, and then adding firmly, 'And anyway, I haven't come all this long way to talk about Marcus...'

'But you don't like Isobel either, do you?' Susie asked slyly.

Her perception was almost frightening, Maggie acknowledged, unable to deny her assertion.

'Have you got a boyfriend?' Susie asked her, changing the subject, and Maggie shook her head quellingly.

'No, and I don't intend to discuss my private life with you, Susie. You asked me to come and I'm here, and while I'll do all I can to try to persuade

Marcus to let you stay at home, I can't promise to
be successful. However, *you* must promise *me* that
if I'm not, you won't try to do anything to hurt
Marcus or to...'

'To hurt him? as if I would!' Susie was immediately indignant and Maggie shook, remembering how once she would have replied just as passionately.

'You may not think of it as hurting him if you
try to break his engagement, but it will,' Maggie
told her quietly, and then added thoughtfully, 'Are
you really so sure you don't want to go to boarding-
school? They can be great fun, and wouldn't it be
better to be there than to stay here and be unhappy?'

'No,' Susie told her stubbornly, but it was the
tears in her eyes and not her vehemence that weak-
ened Maggie's heart. It had been years since they
had last met and yet immediately there was a bond
between them, and it seemed the most natural thing
in the world to open her arms and hold the coltish
teenage body in them, while Susie sobbed out her
frustration and fear.

'Darling, I wish there was something I could
do...but I'm not your guardian and Marcus is...'

'There is something,' Susie told her, sniffling and
pushing her damp hair out of her eyes. '*You* could
stay here and look after us, and then Isobel
wouldn't have any excuse for sending us away...'

'Stay here?' Maggie was stunned, and at first completely lost for words. 'But, Susie, I can't do that...'

'Why not? You could work just as easily up here as you could in London, and you said yourself you don't have a boyfriend or anything...'

It came to Maggie as she listened to her that this was what Susie had wanted all along, that she had had the whole thing worked out, and she looked at her cousin with grim respect. She had forgotten just how Machiavellian and single-minded in their determination teenage girls could be, not hampered, as the more mature were, by the ambiguous gift of being able to see other points of view that might contrast with their own, and she surely, more than anyone else, ought to have remembered...ought to have known the dangers of that single-mindedness.

'Susie, it just isn't possible.'

'You don't have to stay forever... Just a few months, just until we can find a proper housekeeper to look after us. You see, since Mrs Nesbitt had to leave, no one wants to come and work here, because Marcus gets so bad-tempered, and Isobel is so horrid to them, always poking her nose in where it isn't wanted. Please stay, Maggie. We need you.'

'We need you.' How sweet a temptation it was to give in. Deep in her heart Maggie knew there was nothing she wanted more than to stay here, to stay close to...to her family, she told herself, ignoring the betraying lurch of her heart. She couldn't do it, though. Marcus would never let her, and even if he did, it could only be a temporary solution. Sooner or later he and Isobel would marry, and when they did...

Lost in a confusing maze of thoughts, she heard Susie say something and automatically nodded, and then to her shock she heard her give a whoop of pleasure and get to her feet, saying, 'You will? I knew you would! Just wait until I tell Marcus.'

And she danced out of the room before Maggie could stop her, leaving her to race down the stairs after her, and arrive out of breath at the study door just as Susie bounced through it and announced happily, 'Marcus, guess what... Maggie's going to stay and look after us, so that we don't need to go to boarding-school. Isn't that great?'

From outside the room, Maggie heard Marcus's grimly furious, 'Oh, she is, is she?'

And out of nowhere, like a whirlwind conjured up out of nothing to devastate everything that lay in its path, came a thrill of anger so intense that she was through the door and in the room before she realised she had moved, her voice throbbing with the force of her emotions as she announced fatally, 'Yes, I am, and before you start, there's nothing you can do about it, Marcus. This *is* still my home, just as it is the girls'.'

At Marcus's side, Susie started and looked up at

him as though about to speak, but his hand on her arm restrained her.

'I take it that nothing I can say or do will make you change your mind?'

'Nothing,' she replied fiercely, and it was only as the sound of her refusal died away on the tense air of the room that she realised that she had just deliberately closed her last escape route and that she was trapped. Trapped into staying…trapped into living here with Marcus…trapped in a situation she would have given the earth to avoid.

Fear flashed through her eyes and, as her gaze was drawn to focus on Marcus's grim face, she saw in the cynical smile he gave her that he had seen her fear.

'I've got several phone calls I need to make,' she told him coldly, her chin tilting, only her pride keeping her standing where she was instead of flee-ing.

What would he say if he knew that she had got herself into this mess more out of desire to protect him…to prevent him from suffering the trauma of a broken engagement a second time, than anything else? Would he even believe it? To judge from the look he was giving her, it hardly seemed likely.

CHAPTER FOUR

OF THE two sisters, Susie was very evidently the more forceful, Maggie reflected, listening without appearing to to the conversation between the two girls as they helped her to prepare supper.

She had been appalled to discover that, since Marcus's accident, they had been virtually living on tinned and frozen food, neither girl, it seemed, having been taught to cook—something which Maggie intended to rectify just as soon as she possibly could. She was all for her sex forging its way in the world of commerce instead of being relegated to the supportive role of housewife and mother, but she saw no virtue in the girls' inability to put together a simple meal.

As she remembered how painstakingly her own mother and then theirs had passed on their domestic skills to her, she could have wept for all that Susie and Sara were missing. *Why* had it not occurred to her before that she might be needed here? That she might in some small way be able to repay the love and kindness she had received from her aunt and uncle after her own parents' death by passing them on to their daughters?

Because she had been blind to everything but her own anguish…her own fear…her own inability to find the slightest excuse for what she had done.

All these years she had suffered nightmares of horrendous proportions in which she was forced by Marcus to confront the past and all that it held, and yet now that she was here he had made no reference to it. It was almost as though in some way he too preferred to forget what had happened. She could never forget…never…

'What are you doing?' Susie asked her curiously, interrupting her painful reverie.

'Making pastry for a steak and kidney pie,' she told her obligingly. She had found the tin of meat in one of the cupboards and, remembering the mouthwatering pastry her aunt used to make, had decided to use it to make the tinned meat a little more appetising. Marcus had always loved his mother's steak and kidney pie, and the first time she had made one he had praised it generously, despite the fact that it had not rivalled her aunt's.

'But why are you doing that?' Sara asked her as she skilfully dabbed small pieces of butter on to the pastry she had rolled out.

'Because this is how you make puff pastry,' Maggie told her, and then asked thoughtfully, 'Didn't Mrs Nesbitt make it this way?'

'She always used to buy frozen pastry. She said making it herself was a waste of time,' Sara informed her, adding, 'She wasn't a very good cook, was she, Susie?'

'She was all right… Better than Mrs Bakes…and better than Isobel.'

'Who was Mrs Bakes?' Maggie asked, deliberately ignoring this reference to Isobel, and the challenge she could see in Susie's eyes. She had the uncomfortable feeling that she was being manoeuvred very cleverly by the older girl, but dismissed the thought, telling herself that she was becoming neurotic.

'She was our housekeeper after Mrs Nesbitt left. She didn't stay long, though.'

'No, after Marcus had his accident he was really grumpy, and when he complained about her coffee she told him she wasn't standing for any more and that she was going,' Susie told her with relish.

'And since then there hasn't been a housekeeper, is that it?'

'Marcus advertised, but couldn't find anyone suitable. We're too far out from the village for someone without their own transport, and he really wanted someone to live in so that they could keep an eye on us. Why are you doing that?' she asked curiously, watching Maggie work.

'Because…because this is how your mother taught me to cook,' Maggie told her.

Did she? Tell us about her, Maggie. What was she like?'

'Yes, tell us,' Sara begged, echoing her older sister.

Maggie looked at them in some surprise. 'Hasn't Marcus told you? I only lived here for a few years, you know.'

'Well, he has...but you know what he's like,' Susie commented. 'Men don't understand really, do they?' she said with an earnest maturity that made Maggie's lips twitch a little.

'I'm sure Marcus would if you explained just what you wanted to know and why,' she said firmly, subduing a combined urge to laugh and cry at the same time. Marcus had loved his mother very dearly, but he had been adult when the girls were born and his memories of her would be those of a solitary and mature little boy remembering a very young mother whom he had almost exclusively to himself.

The woman she remembered, on the other hand, had been wise, with the experience of her forty-odd years of living. She had been both a mother and a wife, a woman striving hard to balance all the different aspects of her life.

She had been very interested in antique china, Maggie remembered, and very knowledgeable about it.

As she worked, she tried to communicate to the girls her memories of their mother.

'She loved gardening,' she told them. 'She used to spend a lot of time in the kitchen garden. She grew all her own vegetables, I remember, and fruit. We used to spend weeks in the late summer and early autumn bottling and freezing.'

'I like gardening,' Sara told her, 'but John, who comes in twice a week to look after the grounds, likes to be left on his own.'

'Tell us some more,' Susie pressed, elbows on the table, hands cupping her face as she stared at Maggie. The heat from the kitchen had flushed her normally pale skin, and an errant lock of hair had curled forwards to brush her cheek. Maggie pushed it out of the way automatically, watching the pleasure come and go in the young face at her instinctive action. How starved these girls must have been of all the things she had taken for granted, she thought guiltily. It was true that she had lost her parents, but all her life until she left home she had been surrounded by love and warmth…had never doubted that she was cared for and cherished. In that startled look of pleasure in Susie's grey eyes she had seen more clearly than any amount of words could convey how desperately her cousins wanted her to stay…wanted her to love them.

'I should have come back before.'

She wasn't conscious of saying the words out

loud until a harsh voice from the kitchen door answered her rawly, 'So why the hell didn't you?'

Her head snapped round, shock rounding her eyes as she saw Marcus standing in the doorway.

'Marcus, Maggie has just been telling us about Mum,' Susie told him excitedly, completely ignoring his question. 'She's been telling us about the garden…and freezing things.'

'Yes, and she's been showing us how Mum used to make pastry,' Sara added.

As she saw the look in his eyes, Maggie's heart went out to him. She ached to go up to him and touch him, to tell him that he was not to blame, that he could not have known how important these things would be to them. That he, manlike, was scarcely likely to have noticed all of his mother's domestic expertise, her gift for turning a house into a home, other than to simply take the comforts she provided very much for granted.

Instead she quelled the urge and said quietly instead, 'It isn't just boys who need an adult to pattern themselves on, you know.'

And then she went white with shock and self-disgust as she remembered that, but for her, Marcus would long ago have provided them with a feminine role-model in the shape of his wife.

What had happened to her, that long-ago girl to whom he had been going to get engaged? It was scarcely the kind of question she could ask. Had she, like Isobel, heard of her own crush on Marcus?

Looking backwards did no good at all. She couldn't alter what had happened, no matter how much she might wish it.

'Supper won't be long,' she told Marcus in a stifled voice, turning her head away from him and concentrating on her pastry-making.

'Good. Afterwards, I'd like a word with you in the study.'

There was a tense silence, into which Susie jumped, saying defiantly, 'You aren't going to try to persuade Maggie not to stay, are you, Marcus?' When he made no reply, she added desperately, 'Sara and I want her to stay. That's why I wrote to her. Oh, why do grown-ups have to be so difficult?' she added crossly. 'Everyone knows that you and Maggie quarrelled and that she ran away, but whenever I ask anyone why, they all try to pretend they haven't heard. If you did quarrel, why can't you make it up again? After all, that's what you're always telling us to do.'

She had to say something. She couldn't let this go on, Maggie thought frantically. Not with Marcus standing there looking as though he had been turned to stone, his face almost bone-white, his eyes blind and staring right through her.

'We didn't quarrel, Susie,' she said quietly. 'I did something very, very wrong indeed...and...' Help-lessly she looked towards Marcus, silently begging for his help.

'You're quite right, Susie,' he said heavily, limping over to the table and putting his arm round the girl's thin shoulders. 'In actual fact I wanted Maggie to come home a long time ago, and I promise you that, now that she is here, I'm not going to drive her away. Shouldn't you be making a start on your homework, by the way?' he asked drily.

The girls left the kitchen with reluctance, and as the door closed behind them Maggie had a cowardly impulse to call them back. She didn't want to be left alone with Marcus, not right now when her emotions were threatening to overwhelm her. The sound of his voice saying that he had wanted her to come home, in that husky, almost despairing way, had completely undermined her.

'There was no need for you to say that,' she told him shakily. 'I wasn't going to leave anyway...and they'll find out sooner or later that you don't really want me here.'

'Is that why you came back, Maggie...because you knew I wouldn't want you?'

Her face flamed.

'Of course not... I'm not a child, Marcus,' she told him indignantly. 'Neither am I so petty or small-minded as to...' She broke off, flushing even harder as she saw the way he was looking at her. 'All right, I know you must find that hard to believe after what I did...oh, hell, haven't I paid enough for that?' she demanded in a tortured voice. The feelings she had fought to hold at bay ever since her arrival were completely overwhelming her. 'What I did was wrong...terribly wrong...but don't you think I've suffered for it...don't you realise?' She broke off, gritting her teeth and tensing every muscle against the plea she longed to make. She was no longer a child and Marcus her mentor; he could no longer remove all her hurts with his touch and his love. These were wounds she had to bear for herself...wounds she fully deserved.

'I came here because of Susie's letter,' she told him unsteadily when she had herself under control. 'That's all...not out of malice or spite...not for any reason other than because I felt she and Sara needed me.'

Another minute and she would be in floods of tears, and that was the last thing she wanted. She bit down hard on her lip...too hard, she realised as she tasted the rust-salt taste of her own blood and realised what she had done. She touched the small wound with her tongue.

'They do need you.'

The quiet admission stunned her. She stood where she was, her mouth half open, her eyes registering her amazement.

'It won't be for long,' she assured him when she

had got over her astonishment. 'By the time you and Isobel get married...'

An odd look crossed his face. A spasm of something that could almost have been pain. Was it because he knew how much the two girls disliked his fiancée?

'That won't do,' he told her quietly. 'Susie is sixteen, Sara fourteen. If you're serious about making a commitment to them, it's going to have to be for something more like four years than four months...'

'Four years?'

He smiled grimly.

'Yes. Think about it, Maggie, and then after dinner we'll have a talk.'

When he probably expected her to back down, to say that she wasn't prepared to give up four years of her life, Maggie realised sickly as he left the room. Oh, he was clever, she had to give him that. He thought he'd found the ideal way of getting rid of her without arousing the girls' antagonism. He was going to make *her* do the leaving, just as he had done before. She swallowed down the sobs of pure rage building in her throat. This wasn't the time to give way to the feelings burning inside her. She needed to stay calm and controlled...she needed to think.

Four years! But what did it matter...four or forty? There was nothing for her in London. *This* was her home. She already knew she would never marry. But living here meant that she would be constantly tormented by the sight of Marcus himself...by her memories...by her feelings.

She checked herself abruptly. What feelings? She had no feelings left...for Marcus or any other man. She was immune to the emotional and physical impact of any man, incapable of responding to them in any way at all.

So why had she been in this constant turmoil ever since she arrived?

Because of her own guilt, she told herself angrily. That was why. Nothing more.

BECAUSE she wasn't sure where they normally ate and didn't want to disturb either the girls' concentration on their homework or invade Marcus's privacy in his study, Maggie laid the table for supper in the kitchen, using the dinner service on the old-fashioned dresser.

In Marcus's mother's day, supper, or more properly dinner, had always been served and eaten with proper formality in the dining-room, but since tonight's meal was rather a sparse affair Maggie didn't feel it warranted the faded splendour of the Edwardian dining-room with its crimson paper and heavy mahogany furniture.

She had managed to find time to ring Lara and

tell her that she was staying on. Lara had been somewhat disturbingly unsurprised.

'Some day I'm going to make you tell me more about this stepcousin of yours,' she had warned her. 'And don't bother saying there's nothing to tell. When you mentioned his name, you looked just as you used to look when you told Dad you didn't have any family.'

Maggie had blushed a little as she denied her friend's allegation. It was true that, when she first lived with Lara and her father, she had told them she had no family, but later, when she had learned to trust them, she had admitted the truth...or at least some of it. She had kept back the exact reason why she had left, and once he'd realised that no force on earth was going to get her to either confide in them or go back, John Philips had stopped pressing her. She had been lucky to find such a refuge, she acknowledged now as she went to call the others to supper; even now it made her skin crawl to think of the fates that could have befallen her. Had Marcus ever wondered, ever worried...? She stopped herself from following such unprofitable lines of thought. Marcus owed her nothing. He had trusted her and she had abused and betrayed that trust. She had...

Noisy footsteps in the passage reminded her that the past was dead, and Susie and Sara hurried into the kitchen together.

'Smells good,' Sara exclaimed with a smile as she went to sit down. Neither of them made any reference to the fact that they were eating in the kitchen. Maggie had prepared a tray for Marcus, thinking he might prefer the privacy of his study, well away from her, but as she was getting it ready he came into the kitchen and frowned down at it.

'Not eating with us?' he asked her caustically.

She flushed. 'The tray was for you…I thought…'

'Well, don't,' he told her abruptly, and then added under his breath so that the girls couldn't hear, 'Much as you might want to pretend I don't exist, Maggie, I'm afraid I do. If I want to have my meals on my own, you may rest assured that I shall tell you.'

His sarcastic rebuke made her angry. An anger she had no right to feel, she reminded herself as she watched the girls enjoying their food, and pushed her own miserably around her plate.

'Not eating?' Marcus queried, raising an eyebrow.

'I…I'm not hungry. I was wondering if the kitchen garden still exists,' she added hurriedly, uncomfortably aware of the narrow-eyed scrutiny he was giving her slender frame. Did he think she was too thin? Was he comparing her slender frame with Isobel's far more lush curves? Where once she would have been delighted to have his attention on her, to have his gaze on her, now she was made awkward and miserable by his scrutiny, bleakly aware of how dangerously vulnerable he could still make her feel. Now, though, there was no sexual frisson of pleasure in the knowledge, only a cold and nauseous burden of guilt and misery.

'In a way. It's very overgrown. Why?'

'I had to use frozen vegetables tonight, and I couldn't help remembering how your mother always had fresh things.'

'Well, there's no reason why it shouldn't be resuscitated, if that's what you want,' he told her, surprising her. 'When John comes tomorrow, I'll have a word with him. Get him to make a start on clearing out the weeds. We might not get much from it this summer, but next year...'

'Oh, yes...and we could help you,' Sara interrupted, her eyes shining. 'We could make jam like you said Mum used to.'

'Yes,' Maggie agreed softly, touched by the enthusiasm in the younger girl's voice. 'We'll do that. In fact, we could make some this autumn. We'll go blackberrying,' she promised them, 'and see what we can find.'

From the way they all cleaned their plates, even Marcus, it seemed that her cooking was a success, Maggie reflected, as she offered to make some coffee and apologised for the lack of any dessert.

'Girls, you can both help Maggie with the washing-up,' Marcus announced firmly. Once or twice during the meal, watching him listening to something one or other of the girls had been telling him about their day, Maggie could almost have imagined herself back in the past, and then, as though conscious of her concentration, he would turn and look at her and all her guilt and misery would come rushing back.

Now, as he pushed back his chair and stood up, she could see that he looked tired and strained. And no wonder; those plaster casts couldn't exactly be comfortable.

'Perhaps you'd prefer to have your coffee in the study,' she offered formally.

He looked at her, dark eyebrows lifting.

'Trying to get rid of me again?' he asked *sotto voce* as the girls carried the dirty plates over to the sink.

To her own disgust, she flushed. It was ridiculous, this pale skin of hers that so easily gave her away, betraying every single emotion she felt.

'No,' she told him shortly. 'I just thought you might prefer the comfort of the chairs in there. It can't be easy for you—' she looked at the casts '—heaving all that extra weight around.'

'It isn't,' he agreed shortly, 'and they itch damnably. Actually I *have* got some work to do, if you're sure you don't mind.'

'Isobel won't like that,' Susie commented cheerfully, catching his last comment as she came back for the rest of the dirty dishes. 'She was furious when she found out that Marcus was going to be off his feet for so long. She likes to go out dancing and to parties,' she told Maggie, adding thoughtfully, 'I suppose that's why she didn't want us around, 'cos she'd have to find babysitters and things for us.'

'Susie…' Marcus warned her tetchily, but Susie ignored the warning growl in his voice and tossed her head.

'It isn't my fault if she doesn't like us. Mrs Nesbitt said she only got engaged to you anyway because she'd had a row with her last boyfriend.'

'Susie, I don't think you should repeat gossip,' Maggie intervened hurriedly, not daring to look at Marcus to see how he was reacting to these disclosures. Behind her, she heard Marcus making to get up, and as he did so he staggered a little, suddenly clumsy. She reacted instinctively, reaching out to steady him, surprised to feel the fine tremor racing over his skin as she held on to him to balance him. It was hardly cold enough to merit such a shiver, and then she realised that the muscles beneath her fingers were bunched in tense agony, and as she looked into the too-dark depths of his eyes, she realised that she was the cause of that shudder of revulsion.

She let go of him immediately, her skin burning with acute misery. Of course he would loathe the

very touch of her, but she hadn't thought. She had
simply wanted to help him. Idiotic tears blurred her
eyes and she turned her back on him, hating herself
for her stupidity.

When she had made the coffee, she got Susie to
take it into him. The girls still had homework to
do, and while they did it she busied herself check-
ing on the meagre contents of the cupboards.

Tomorrow whe would have to do some shopping.
She could do it after she had dropped the girls off
at school...which reminded her...

She went upstairs and knocked briefly on the
school-room door before walking in.

'Washing,' she announced briefly. 'I need to
wash some of my own things tomorrow. Lara, my
flatmate, is going to send on the rest of my clothes,
but until they arrive I'm stuck with what I've
brought with me. And while we're on the subject...what kind of routine did Mrs Nesbitt have?'

'Routine?' Susie queried, nibbling the end of her
pen. Her hair needed trimming, Maggie noticed ab-
sently, and perhaps even reshaping in a different
style. Her school skirt was also far too short, almost
indecently so.

'Yes, you know...when did she do the shopping
and the washing? Which days?'

Susie's forehead cleared.

'Oh...oh, she didn't have one. She just did things
when she felt like doing them, didn't she, Sara?'

Maggie was astounded that Marcus had put up with such a ramshackle state of affairs, especially when she remembered the way in which his mother had run the house.

It seemed that she had taken on a bigger task than she had imagined. She would be needed for four years, Marcus had warned her, and suddenly her mouth quirked in unexpected amusement. Four years to teach them all the feminine skills it had taken her half a lifetime to learn? Well, why not? It would give her a purpose in life...a cause...a reason for being. It would answer a need in her which had remained hungry and unappeased for far too long. She would enjoy being a surrogate mother to these cousins of hers, she recognised on a sudden shaft of self-knowledge. They would fill the space in her heart left empty by the children of her own she would never have. She was needed here and she needed to be here, and she wasn't going to let anyone or anything drive her away.

CHAPTER FIVE

IT WAS almost ten o'clock before she was free to make her way to the study in response to Marcus's earlier command. The reason for the delay had nothing to do with any reluctance on her part to face Marcus alone, she reassured herself as she went downstairs.

During term-time the girls were apparently expected to start preparing for bed at about ten o'clock unless some special occasion necessitated them staying up later, and she had, of course, needed to find out from them as much about their everyday routine as she could, which had kept her upstairs in the school-room with them until almost ten.

Their rooms were not on the same floor as hers, but one floor above, the nursery floor, where they had apparently been quite happy to remain. They had separate rooms, but shared a bathroom and a room which had originally been their playroom, but which they now referred to as the 'den'. It was comfortably furnished, with an ancient, sagging settee and two equally old chairs, and although Maggie's housewifely eye noticed that the same film of dust so much in evidence downstairs covered this room as well, she remembered enough of her own teenage years not to make any comment.

Pop records and tapes jostled quite happily for space alongside more classical music; a pair of tennis racquets in their presses were leaning up against one of the walls; what looked like at least half a dozen assorted pairs of tennis shoes were discarded next to them.

Both girls rode and played tennis, but it was Sara, the younger sister, who had the musical ear, Susie explained to her as she talked to them, drawing them out about their hobbies and how they spent their spare time.

It was obvious from their conversation that they both thoroughly enjoyed attending their local convent school. Although they were in different classes, they both seemed to have a large circle of friends, certainly far more than she could ever remember having, and in fact they were both extremely well-rounded and mature young people. Far more so than she remembered being at the same age.

It appalled her now to recollect that at sixteen, Susie's age, she had been so firmly convinced of her love for Marcus that her whole world had narrowed down so that she had virtually excluded everyone else from it.

The death of her parents when she was just entering her teens, the fact that she had been too shy to make many new friends at her new school, the shocking deaths of her aunt and uncle, her grandfather's poor health...all these things had exacerbated the situation, but the original fault had lain with her, a massive fault in her personality, which had enabled her to blinker herself to reality.

She recalled abruptly one hot summer's day some time after the death of her aunt and uncle. Marcus was working in the garden, shirt off, the sunlight playing on the hard muscles of his back and arms. She had been sitting watching him, totally absorbed in greedily filling her senses with the sight and scent of him...so much so that she hadn't realised they had a visitor until Mrs Hayes, the then vicar's wife, had touched her on her shoulder.

She remembered how she had spun round in shock and anger, not wanting anyone to interrupt her precious moments with Marcus. She had given the vicar's wife a fierce look of resentment as she stood up, and it was only now, with the maturity and wisdom of her much older self, that she was able to realise that the look she had surprised on Mrs Hayes's face had been one of intense concern. A kind-hearted woman, she had called quite frequently in those early days of her aunt and uncle's death, Maggie remembered. She had even suggested that Maggie might like to stay at the vicarage for a while. The older woman had perhaps seen the danger which Maggie herself had been totally oblivious to, in her intense devotion to Marcus.

She remembered how she had burst into tears the moment Marcus had suggested the visit, demanding to know why he wanted to send her away. He had always hated to see her crying, and she had known it and played on that knowledge, she admitted wryly, and of course the visit had never materialised. Perhaps her whole life would have been different if it had. She might have found a good friend in the vicar's wife, and that friendship might have distracted her from her emotional dependence on Marcus.

Thank goodness neither Susie nor Sara showed any signs of sharing her own teenage intensity. They were much better adjusted than she had ever been...everything that parents always hoped their teenage daughters might be, although she suspected they were quite capable of the odd tantrum and sulk now and again.

At the moment she and they were very much in the honeymoon period of their relationship. It remained to be seen how they would get along when they had had more opportunity to get to know one another. She had fortunately had some experience of teenage girls, having worked for a brief space of time some years earlier at a private school in London, taking the art classes during the illness of the regular art teacher. That experience had helped her to see how very abnormal in many ways her own teenage life had been, centred exclusively as it had been on Marcus and Deveril.

That had been her fault and not his. There had been opportunities for her to make friends, but she had shunned them all, so very protective and possessive of her relationship with Marcus, so determined that one day he was going to look at her and return her love, that she had deliberately excluded everyone else from her life. That was why it had been so easy for her to slip from reality into fantasy…into a world where Marcus did, in fact, already love her…and not as a child, but as a woman. And once she had found the door to that fantasy world, she had opened it more and more often, so that there had eventually come a time when in her subconscious mind the fantasy became fact.

She now saw that time, that experience as a dark pit from which she had only just managed to drag herself free. She shuddered a little as she closed the girls' sitting-room door behind her and headed for the stairs. What would have happened to her if it hadn't been for the catalyst of Marcus announcing his engagement? Would she have gone on deluding herself until eventually… Her mouth went dry as she contemplated the consequences of such folly.

It was two floors down to the study. It had been in that room that Marcus had told her that he was going to get engaged, and with those words had broken the spell of her fantasy world for her.

She had screamed out at him that it was impossible, that he loved *her*, and her grandfather, passing outside the room, had come in, and she had turned to him and begged him to stop Marcus from betraying her.

She stood at the top of the stairs with her hand on the worn wooden rail, lost in the past. She had said things that even now she couldn't bear to recall…made allegations in the furnace of her passion and pain which, had they been true… She shuddered coldly. But of course they hadn't been true, and Marcus had forced her to admit as much. And she, unable to bear not just the burden of the truth but the added and far heavier burdens of her grandfather's shock and Marcus's hatred, had fled rather than face up to reality.

Reality had its own way of making itself felt, though, and in London she had been forced to come to terms with what she had done…to leave behind her comfortable fantasy world and see life as it really was.

She didn't blame Marcus for what he had done. She never had. The blame and the fault were hers, and though there had been many, many times when she had ached to come home, when she would have given her soul for Marcus's forgiveness and warm smile, she had forced herself to remain in exile until now.

Her concern for Susie had brought her north on a fast-flowing flood of emotion which was now starting to ebb, leaving her feeling vulnerable and defenceless. In the heat of the moment she had told Marcus that she intended to stay, virtually challenging him to stop her.

The house was centrally heated, the evening balmy and warm, but she was still shivering as she reached the bottom of the stairs and made her way to the study door.

It was closed, and she rapped on it tentatively.

'Yes?' Marcus looked up, frowning as she walked in, his voice terse. His desk was covered with files. He had always worked hard, first as a junior partner in the estate agents and auctioneers he had joined after leaving university, and then when he'd set up his own estate agency.

The harshness of the desk lamp illuminated the lines of tension on his face, cut sharply in grooves that ran from his nose to his mouth. Lines which were new to her, she recognised sadly.

'You wanted to see me,' she reminded him.

A gas fire burned in the Adam grate and she went over to it, holding out her hands to the flames, even though they gave off little heat.

'Cold?' he asked her sharply.

She was, but not in any way that had anything

to do with the temperature of the air. No, the chill eating away inside her came from years of guilt and pain…from knowing just how much she had wronged him…from carrying the anguish of remorse and regret as her constant burden.

'Not really. I thought for a moment the fire was real.'

'Mrs Nesbitt, our last housekeeper, told me that there was no way she was going to clean out coal fires, so I had that installed. It's far from an adequate substitute.'

'It looks effective, though.'

'Maybe, but as you've just discovered, there's nothing more disappointing than discovering that your eyes have deceived you into believing an attractive and welcoming exterior means there's going to be something equally warm behind it.'

He sounded very tired, and as he got up from behind his desk he half stumbled, bumping into it, and sending a silver photograph frame clattering down on to its wooden surface. As he picked it up, Maggie saw the photograph it held and her lungs seized up in a paroxysm of shock.

It was her. Taken on her seventeenth birthday, a formal photograph commissioned by her grandfather.

'You've still got that,' she whispered huskily, the words scraping her tense muscles.

'Yes,' Marcus replied tersely, without looking at

her. 'It serves to remind me...' He broke off and looked directly at her, shocking her into frozen immobility. She had forgotten the effect those hypnotic grey eyes could have... She had forgotten how it could feel when he looked at her like that...as though he could see right through to her soul.

Once she had fantasised about seeing those eyes grow warm and then burn with desire. Had mentally visualised them darkening with passion, as he held her and touched her, her imaginings as wild and feverish as only those of teenage girls can be...her knowledge of sex gleaned more from what she had read than anything she had personally experienced.

And she didn't have much more experience than that now, she reminded herself grimly. The only difference was that now she realised that there was far more to loving someone than sexual desire.

'So you still do that?'

The harsh words shocked her, and she focused abruptly on him, staring at him in confusion.

'What?'

'Do you really not know? It used to infuriate me, that ability of yours to drift off into your private world where no one could follow you. I thought you must have grown out of it.'

Her face flamed the guilt that was never far away from surfacing painfully. 'I have,' she told him shortly. 'What do you want to talk to me about,

Marcus? It's getting late, and I have to be up early in the morning to drive the girls to school. I'm hoping to get something organised on a rota basis once I've found my feet, but I thought it might be an idea to see if I can arrange to see the headmistress and have a chat with her. What's she like?'

'So you still intend to go through with it?' Marcus demanded ignoring her last question.

Maggie tensed. This was it. This was what she had been dreading...why she had been putting off this confrontation all evening.

'Hadn't I already made that clear?' she answered obliquely, feeling her nerves tighten when he remained silent, staring, not at her, but out of the window into the dusky twilight of the June garden.

'I thought perhaps once you'd had time to reflect you might...'

'Change my mind? No, Marcus,' she told him, shaking her head. 'Susie and Sara need me here. Even you can't deny that. They don't like Isobel, and from what I've heard her say I judge that she doesn't care much for them...' She saw that he was about to interrupt and held up her hand, continuing challengingly, 'You're going to deny it! *Why*— when we both know that it's true? Look at it this way: my staying here to look after the girls will free you and Isobel to make your own lives.'

'Away from here?' Marcus asked her silkily.

'Did I say that?'

'By implication, but my life is here, Maggie. My home is here, and I intend that it is going to remain here.'

'That's something you should take up with Isobel, not me,' Maggie told him unwisely. 'After all, she's the one who's going to be your wife.'

The minute she said the words, she knew it was a mistake. They were too dangerous…too evocative of all that lay between them…

She saw a shadow pass across Marcus's face and wondered if he was thinking of that other girl who should have held that role. The girl she had never met. He must have loved her a great deal indeed not to have married for so long. Why hadn't he married her once she herself had gone? These were questions she could never ask him. The old intimacy and easiness between them had gone forever, and in its place was a savage hostility which both of them tried to mask but which constantly flared into life. And she was going to have to live with the knowledge of that hostility. She was going to have to live side by side with Marcus and Isobel… She was going to have to see them building a life together…having a family…and suddenly she wondered what on earth she had done.

'See, you're not as convinced you're doing the right thing as you pretend,' Marcus pounced, seeing the doubt fill her eyes. 'Taking on the responsibility of parenting two teenage girls is no easy task…as I know.'

'So do I,' Maggie told him fiercely. 'I'm not seventeen any more, Marcus. I'm an adult…a woman. Or are you, oh, so subtly, trying to imply that you don't consider me a morally fit person to have charge of them?'

The tension was almost tangible now, and Marcus was obviously as aware of it as she was, because he limped over to the french windows and pushed them open angrily, standing in the cool waft of evening air, staring out over the grounds. He was silent for a long time and then, when he did speak, his voice was so raw and low that she had trouble hearing it. Automatically she walked closer to him, trying to catch what he was saying.

'Maggie…*think…think* what you're doing.' He swung round, catching her off guard, less than half the length of the desk between them, his eyes brilliant and glittering oddly, the pupils slightly enlarged. Every bone in his face seemed to be tensed in fierce pressure, and Maggie had a tremendous awareness both of his power and his emotional control. She had the vivid impression that he would like to do her violence, and that he was only stopping himself with great difficulty.

'I *have* thought,' she told him shakily. 'And I'm staying. You can't make me leave, Marcus.'

It was the wrong thing to say. He closed the gap

between them, saying harshly, 'Can't I? We'll see about that.'

And then, shockingly, he had taken hold of her, her body suddenly frighteningly fragile as she felt the pressure of his grip, threatening her ribcage.

'What have you really come back for, Maggie?' he demanded thickly, his breath warm against her skin. She wanted to pull away from him, but she was too conscious of the weight of his casts to push him hard in case she damaged them, and besides, he had her trapped between his body and the desk.

His body... She drew an agonised breath of shock as he shifted his weight and leaned heavily into her. He was aroused physically in a way that was totally unfamiliar to her, and where once she would have swooned with pleasure at the knowledge, now she was sickened by it...knowing that it sprang not from desire but from anger.

She felt the heat of his breath graze her ear and knew that he was going to kiss her. She turned her head away from him and demanded, 'Stop this, Marcus. I know you must hate me...I know you must want to punish me for what I did, but not...'

'Then if you *know* it, why don't you stop fighting me and accept your punishment?' he jeered harshly.

She could feel in the heavy rise and fall of his chest the effort it was costing him to breathe. One sharp push and she could probably unbalance him... As though he picked up her thoughts, he pushed her back harder against the desk, pinning her there.

'You owe me this,' he told her angrily, and then his free hand slid into her hair, tightening almost painfully in it, holding her immobile while his mouth savaged hers in a kiss of such violence that she could scarcely believe it was happening.

During her years in London she had dated many men. A goodnight kiss was as far as she allowed them to get, and over the years she imagined she had experienced every kind of kiss there was, but now, shockingly, she realised she was wrong.

As she fought to deny the angry domination Marcus was forcing upon her, he grated against her swollen lips, 'Open your mouth. Open it, Maggie, or I'll make you.' And when she still refused, her body trembling with shock and fear, his fingers tightened their grip and he whispered savagely, 'Remember what you said to your grandfather...that you and I were already lovers...that I had taken you to my bed and initiated you into every art there is... You owe me this, Maggie.'

And, because her muscles had suddenly turned weak and fluid at the mention of the past, she obeyed him, limply and automatically, a rag doll in his arms while he savaged her mouth until she could bear it no more and the salt tears ran down her cheeks, stinging the tender, bruised flesh of her lips.

He released her then, staggering back from her as though she had indeed pushed him. He looked dazed and white, his eyes unfocused, his muscles clenched as though he himself couldn't believe what he had done.

When he lifted his hand and reached out to touch her sore mouth, she jerked away.

'Oh, Maggie...'

'You aren't going to make me go away, Marcus,' she told him thickly, and then added quietly, 'And if you ever touch me like that again, I promise you I'll go straight to Isobel and tell her exactly what kind of man she's marrying.'

He looked like a man who'd been put on the rack, she recognised, her own emotions running too strongly and turbulently for her to recognise the anguish that darkened his eyes as his hand fell away and he said rawly, 'Maggie, I'm sorry. I just...'

'Wanted to punish me. Yes, I know.'

She had to get out of this room before she broke apart completely...before she broke down in front of him and sobbed out her pain and grief.

As she turned for the door, her sight was blinded by the bitterness of her tears. All these years she had kept in the secret places of her heart an image of Marcus as the perfect lover. All these years she had rejected other men because they were not him, and now, shockingly, in one brutal kiss he had shown her how far her dreams had been from reality.

She found her way back upstairs more by instinct than anything else, suddenly realising she was standing in her bedroom without having any real idea of how she had got there.

She hadn't closed the curtains, and outside the sky was that intense shade of dark blue lighting to pale turquoise that seemed to be a feature of the short Northern summer night.

She had no idea what time it was. She could have been in the study hours or seconds. Stars made pinpoints of light overhead. Her window was open, and through it she could smell the rich scent of the old-fashioned climbing rose on the wall outside.

It was a French rose, brought home, so the tale went, by the Deveril who managed to attach himself to the court of the young Mary, Queen of Scots, and planted, where it had eventually flourished, in the gardens of the original Pele tower.

The foundations of that tower still existed in the grounds, and when the new house had been built the new bride had insisted on planting an offshoot of that original rose against its walls...for good luck, or so the story went.

Her husband, who had little time for such sentiment, but was mindful of his wife's handsome dowry, let her have her way just as long as the rose was not allowed to spoil the handsome proportions of the new mansion, and so it had been planted here at the back of the house.

It had been her father who had told her that story, Maggie remembered numbly. She closed the curtains, but left the window open. How clean the air was up here...she had forgotten.

She crossed to the dressing-table and switched on the lamp, exclaiming in shock as she saw how swollen and bruised her mouth looked.

As he'd tasted her tears, Marcus had sworn savagely against its softness. She could have sworn that when he released her he had been as shocked by his behaviour as she was herself. She had always had a good deal too much imagination, she acknowledged bitterly, as she used some moisturiser to soothe the worst of the sting.

If she bathed her skin with cold water, with luck by tomorrow morning most of the bruising would have gone down.

Even now she found it hard to believe what had happened. She had known Marcus would not welcome her back, of course. How could he? She had expected objections...reasoned arguments, sarcasm, and even a downright refusal to let her stay; but the last thing she had been prepared for had been that furious kiss.

She slipped off her blouse and skirt and put on her robe over her underclothes, gathering up her toilet-bag. The bathroom was only a little way down the passage, and she was hardly likely to meet anyone, least of all Marcus.

Even so, she was relieved when she was actually inside the bathroom with the door locked safely.

She showered quickly and then spent almost fifteen minutes doing what she could do to control the swelling that made her lips look so full and red. Her hand trembled just a little as she touched antiseptic to the tiny cuts inflicted by Marcus's teeth, and her reflection in the mirror shimmered and danced in front of her as fresh tears filled her eyes.

She refused to let them fall, tensing every muscle until the desire to cry was beaten back. She was not one of those fortunate women who could cry beautifully, and besides, she had surely cried enough tears for one lifetime over Marcus.

When she went back to her room, the lights were still on downstairs and Marcus was presumably still in the study. Her last thought as she drifted off to sleep was that, no matter what Marcus might do, she was not going to leave. Susie and Sara needed her, and she…well, she needed to be needed, she acknowledged sleepily. Good friend though Lara was, she was a very independent person, and long ago, during the early days of their relationship, she had teased Maggie so much about her yearning to provide Lara and her father with the kind of domestic comfort and contentment she herself had

known in her aunt's household that Maggie had
taken the hint and ceased trying to 'mother' them.

'Some women have an instinctive urge to nur-
ture,' John Philips had told her consolingly, sensing
her distress. 'And there's nothing to feel ashamed
of, no matter what Lara might have told you. For
Lara, her career and perhaps ultimately one man
will always dominate her life.' He had smiled
whimsically at her then and added, 'If God chose
to make us all different, who are we to question his
judgement?'

There was that need in her, she recognised
tiredly. In London she had subdued it in forcing
herself to take a more practical attitude, but Lara
still teased her that she could never resist filling the
flat with flowers and their friends with home-made
food. Even in her work the need was there, as nothing gave her more satisfaction than to see a writer's
face light up with pleasure when she had success-
fully captured the essence of their characters in her
illustrations.

It had been a long journey home to this very
special place, and now that she was here... Now
that she was here, she fully intended to stay.

THAT NIGHT she had a dream. It was as familiar to
her as her own reflection, and as it started she had
the dreamer's awareness that it was just a dream
and at the same time the familiar terror of wishing

there was some way she could avoid what was to come.

It always started in the same way. She was in a garden, full of flowers and sunlight. She was happy, filled with joy and anticipation, and the reason for that joy was the man walking towards her, and then suddenly, as he came towards her, he started to blot out the sun, and her joy gave way to fear. She put her hands up in front of her face, as though to ward off something she did not want to see, but he wrenched them away. And then he was shaking her quite violently, his voice booming and rolling like thunder as he demanded inexorably, 'Tell him the truth…tell him the truth.'

In her sleep she moved fretfully, making small, incomprehensible sounds of distress, her forehead pleated in a frown. She tried to protest…to beg for mercy, for he was growing even more angry and her fear increased. And yet, when he released her and turned to walk away, she screamed after him not to go, running after his departing figure.

The garden was walled, though, and, while he passed through the gate let into it, for some reason she could not do so and was left standing there, watching him leave her, tears flooding from her eyes.

Marcus, on his way to bed, heard her crying and paused outside her room, listening for a moment

before pushing open the door and hesitating on the
threshold.

When he realised that Maggie wasn't awake, he
frowned and then approached the bed. She cried out
something, the meaning of the muttered words un-
intelligible, but their anguish so clear that he
flinched as though in reciprocal pain. He saw that
she was crying and, as though unable to stop himself, he bent down and touched her face tentatively.
Her skin felt hot beneath his fingertips, hot and soft.
He had forgotten. He gave a deep shudder, as
though his body was under intense pressure, and
then, completely unable to stop himself, leaned over
the bed, supporting his weight with his good arm,
gently touching his mouth to her tear-stained skin.

As though his touch was a benison, immediately
she stopped crying, her restless movements ceasing.
Straightening up, Marcus stayed watching her
broodingly, until he was sure that she had fallen
into a deep and relaxing sleep.

Looking at her now, with her hair all tangled on
the pillow, her skin innocent of make-up, she
looked hardly any different than she had done as a
seventeen-year-old girl: so many regrets, so much
pain.

As he moved awkwardly towards the door, he
wondered grimly if he would find it as easy to sleep
as she obviously did; somehow he doubted it.

CHAPTER SIX

MAGGIE woke up early, conscious of the most unexpected sense of well-being and peace. She touched her face tentatively and then coloured up angrily. What was the matter with her? she asked herself cynically; did she really believe that, because for the first time in all the years she had been having the dream Marcus had heeded her cries, and had turned round and come back through the gate to hold out his arms to her and to hold her safely in them, it had actually happened?

It struck her as an uncomfortable coincidence that the dream should change so dramatically on the very same night as Marcus had kissed her. Not the kind of kiss she had dreamed of receiving from him as a girl, either.

His kiss had been forced upon her in anger and punishment and yet, for all that, his body had been aroused to passion...just as her senses had been stirred by the same sharp flare of sexual arousal.

She tried to dismiss the thought, knowing that it was an admission she didn't want to acknowledge. She had been so angry at the time that she had been able to ignore that shocking frisson of awareness and need, that almost lemming-like urge to press herself into him and to let herself drown beneath the savage onslaught of his mouth.

She started to shake, tiny tremors raising goosebumps on her skin. It had been so long since she had experienced sexual desire, and never…never with that primitive intensity. As a teenager, she had been as much curious about sex as she was fathoms deep in her fantasy love for Marcus, but now she was a woman, and that fierce thrill of sensation she had felt had been as unmistakable as it was unwanted. As a girl she had spent many, many hours in this room daydreaming about what it would be like to be made love to by Marcus, and then, when her daydreams had trembled over the dangerous edge between imagining and fantasy, she had been so skilled at persuading herself that he loved her that when she lay on her bed, and gave herself to her daydreams, she could almost feel the sensation of his mouth moving on hers…the weight of his body…

Her yearning body had known no inhibitions or barriers, and her reading had supplied her with a vast wealth of detail about the art of making love.

In her imagination Marcus came to her in the cool darkness of the night, opening the door to her room and stepping inside. She was invariably already lying on her bed, clad not in the girlish cotton nightdresses which were the only nightwear she possessed, but in some fine mist of silk, through which the perfection of her flesh glowed and enticed so that Marcus could only stand and stare before reaching to touch her with hands that trembled...or perhaps she would choose to clothe herself in sumptuous satin, which slithered sensuously against her skin as she sat up in bed to question what he was doing in her room.

In these fantasies, Marcus was always the instigator of their lovemaking, while she was the quiescent, all desirable, irresistible siren.

She would get up off the bed and approach him, and Marcus, who in these daydreams was always wearing something far more romantic than the rather prosaic ancient towelling bathrobe he normally favoured, would come towards her, unable to drag his gaze from the pointed thrust of her breasts where they strained against the satin.

As she had daydreamed, so her body, intensely attuned to her thoughts and needs, had reacted, so that it was merely enough for her to imagine Marcus looking at her breasts for them to immediately swell and harden, until her nipples did in fact make small pinpricks of desire against the cotton of her nightdress.

As he looked at her, it was then that he would beg her to allow him to kiss her, slavishly adoring her in a way that the real Marcus with his calm and slightly cynical manner was hardly likely to emulate, and she, while enjoying the tiny thrill of pleasure his need gave her, withheld herself from him, punishing him in her daydreams for his refusal to acknowledge her love for him, to see her as a grown woman and not a child. In these daydreams, it was *she* who was in control…*she* who orchestrated what happened between them.

Of course, after a delicious period of teasing, she always allowed him to have his kiss, and for a while that had sufficed, but as she had grown older, no longer sixteen but on the way to eighteen, so her need had grown, and her knowledge, and there were times when she ached to be alone in her room so that she could be with her fantasy lover—with Marcus.

Now he was no longer content to press chaste kisses to her sixteen-year-old lips, and behind her closed eyelids she felt the heat of his breath searing her skin, following the path of his hands as they slid over her seductively clad body. If she really concentrated, it was almost possible for her to feel his hands cupping her breasts, his fingers eagerly seeking their engorged peaks, but here again she was the one in control and he the supplicant, begging her with feverish words to allow him to touch her.

Of course he was desperate to make love to her, but for some reason, even though she had seen him on any number of occasions stripped to the waist, and even, on one never to be forgotten one, had been standing just outside his bedroom when he emerged from it wearing only a pair of very brief briefs, which had hardly concealed as much as Adam's figleaf, in her imaginings she rarely visualised Marcus's body. It had been her own sensuality which had concerned her…her own needs.

Gradually, as she had drifted deeper and deeper away from reality and into the darkness of her fantasy world, her fevered daydreams of his lovemaking had grown more intense, and almost at will she had been able to conjure up the sensation of his mouth against her breast…against her belly, her body on fire with desire and triumph while he pleaded with her to acknowledge his love for her.

Sometimes, in the early hours after these imaginings, she had woken up tense and aching with an odd sort of pain and an emptiness inside her that made her wish Marcus would hurry up and realise that she was grown up.

Grown up…Maggie sighed and shook her head grimly over her own folly, her face flushed by the vividness and sensuality of her own imagination. Now, of course, she knew that making love meant giving pleasure as well as receiving it. If she were to indulge in those daydreams now, it would not just be Marcus's hands and mouth on her own body that she would want to conjure up, but hers on his. She would...

Aghast, she caught herself up, her skin fiery with heat and shame. What on earth was she doing?

In the village the church clock struck the hour. She had a busy day ahead, and there was little point in wasting time sitting here reliving the past.

On her way downstairs, she paused on the galleried landing to check her reflection in the mirror that hung there. Her mouth no longer looked bruised, but it did look softer than usual, fuller...somehow very vulnerable. A fine tremor ran through her and she turned away from her reflection, determinedly refusing to dwell on last night's confrontation with Marcus.

The staircase was oak, and the balustrade had been carved by Grinling Gibbons. All manner of fantastical creatures peered out on the world from their wooden prison. Bunches of grapes and other fruits were skilfully woven with the arms of the Deverils. As a child, this staircase had fascinated her, these carvings exercising a spell on her imagination which had made her dream at night that the creatures were alive. That had been in the days when she only visited the house with her parents. She sighed faintly, touching the wood with gentle fingers. Dust had gathered on the carvings, spoiling the beauty of the wood. She wondered idly if Mrs Cermitage in the village still made her own beeswax; her aunt had sworn by it, and the wood looked as though it would welcome a good feed.

There was no one else in the kitchen, and, re-membering how little there was in the way of food provisions, Maggie reflected that a shopping trip needed to be very high on her list of priorities. She could drive to Hexham after she had dropped the girls off at school.

She made some fresh coffee and, while she was waiting for it to filter, she started making out a shopping list. Although Marcus had always enjoyed his food, he had always been careful about his diet, and now it showed, she acknowledged, mentally visualising his lean fitness, remembering how hard and muscled his body had felt against her own.

That recollection brought back others, and as she bent back over her shopping list her skin burned.

'Mm—that smells good,' Susie announced, hur-rying into the kitchen.

She was wearing her school uniform. It hadn't changed much since she herself had worn it, Mag-gie acknowledged.

Like the girls, she too had received her schooling privately at a local convent which took pupils of all denominations, just as long as they were girls. Girls worked harder and achieved more without the dis-traction of boys; mixed schooling often led to girls deliberately holding themselves back so as not to appear more intelligent than their male peers, and

Maggie knew that the convent was justly proud of the number of girls who stayed on until the sixth form and went on from there to universities.

Marcus and Sara arrived in the kitchen together, which meant that Maggie was able to get away with offering him a cool 'good morning' under cover of Sara's chatter.

Over breakfast, nothing was said about their interview the previous night. In view of his half-sisters' very obvious delight at having her home, there was very little Marcus *could* say, Maggie acknowledged cynically.

He obviously had a good relationship with them, but he was their guardian as well as their half-brother, and it was obvious to Maggie, listening to the conversation, that he was quite a firm disciplinarian.

Neither of the girls seemed to resent it, though, and since it was equally obvious that he cared very deeply for them Maggie suspected that they had their own way of getting round him when they really wanted to.

Both of them kissed him naturally and affectionately as they gathered up their jackets and schoolbooks.

'Don't let him bully you into leaving when we're gone, Maggie,' Susie warned her, grinning at him. 'He's had a horrid temper since he had his accident.'

'Don't worry,' Maggie told her lightly, focusing on Marcus's shuttered face. 'I'm quite definitely here to stay.'

She saw from the grim way Marcus's mouth tightened that he knew exactly what she meant, but would he also know how much heart-searching had gone into that decision? Probably not. He might even see it as simply a rather childish way of defying and irritating him, but in reality...

In reality, despite her anger over the way he had treated her last night, inwardly she still felt the weight of her guilt. Inwardly she still yearned to wipe out the past and to share with him that closeness they had once known. When he smiled at the girls, she felt so shut out...so cold...so hurt...

Horrified by what she was thinking, she tried to push her thoughts away, hurrying the girls with their preparations and rushing into an unsteady and rather muddled speech about her intentions of making an appointment to see the headmistress, and then going on to do some shopping.

'If you're going shopping, you'll need some money,' Marcus interrupted her, reaching awkwardly into the pocket of the tweed jacket he was wearing.

As he did so, his crutch fell to the floor. Maggie automatically dived towards it at the same time as Marcus himself reached out to rescue it, his unplastered fingers brushing hers as they closed round the crutch.

Instantly her body burned, shocking tingles of sensation racing up her arm. Her heart started to pound frantically, her pulses thudding out a message which she told herself was fear and shock.

'I think I've got enough. We can sort it out when I get back,' she told him huskily, quickly withdrawing from contact with him.

Only when she was safely at the door did she turn to face him and demand rawly, 'I take it I have your permission to tell the school that I shall be taking charge of the girls?'

They had both gone out ahead of her and she could hear their voices ringing on the still summer air outside in the courtyard.

Marcus looked at her steadily for a long time. She held her breath, half expecting another battle.

'Would it make any difference if I withheld it?' he asked at last.

'Not to my decision to stay, no,' Maggie told him, adding quietly, 'but when it comes to what I shall tell other people...' Her face went pale, but she faced him squarely. 'I've learned my lessons well, Marcus. Too well to ever again commit the folly of lying.'

She saw from his sharp intake of breath and darkening gaze that she had caught him off guard. A muscle pulsed in his jaw and she could almost feel the tension invading him as though it were her own.

'Maggie,' he said at last, 'about last night...'

Now it was her turn to experience tension, but she refused to give in to her desire to flee.

'It didn't work, Marcus,' she said instead. 'You can't frighten me into leaving.'

'*Frighten* you...'

An odd look crossed his face, an almost yearning, anguished look that made her heart almost stop beating and her feet propel her four or five steps towards him. And then abruptly she stopped.

Are you crazy? she asked herself mentally, and, turning on her heel, she left before she could do anything even more foolish.

IT WASN'T VERY FAR to the convent school, which was housed in a Victorian mansion some fifteen miles away.

Maggie was a good driver. Marcus had taught her, and she was used to the winding country lanes. Even so, she was surprised to see how much the volume of traffic had increased in the time she had been away. However, they reached the school in good time. Maggie parked the car and, while the girls went off to find their friends, she hurried towards the main door to the school.

Inside it was much as she remembered: the familiar smell of chalk and disinfectant. Black-robed nuns moved silently through the corridors, their faces composed.

She herself had never experienced any kind of vocation, but as she looked at them now she marvelled at their inner serenity.

The secretary's office was a busy jumble of papers and books; the secretary herself, new since Maggie's days as a pupil, smiled warmly at her and asked how she could help.

Maggie explained briefly, and asked if it was possible to make an appointment to see the Reverend Mother.

'I think she could possibly see you now,' she was told. 'If you'd just like to wait while I check.'

The secretary returned almost immediately.

'Yes, she can. If you'd just like to go through.'

Both the room and its occupant had changed since Maggie's day. Reverend Mother was somewhere in her late thirties, a tall, very attractive woman with an air of calm peace and authority about her.

Accepting both a chair and a cup of coffee, Maggie quickly explained the position.

'The two Deveril girls... Yes, I remember hearing that their brother had been injured in an accident. You say you've come home to take charge...' She looked speculatively at Maggie. 'I'm sorry, but I'm not quite sure what relationship...'

'I'm their cousin,' Maggie explained. 'My father

and their father were brothers. My father was the younger brother.'

'I see. So your cousin asked you if you could come home and take charge of the girls.'

'My cousin? I... Oh, I see. Marcus isn't exactly my cousin. His mother had been married before she married my uncle.'

'I see.' She gave Maggie an oddly thoughtful look. 'Well, girls of that age can be rather difficult for a man to bring up on his own.'

Before she left, Maggie had been given a list of the families living close by who had girls at the school, so that she could get in touch with them, with a view to sharing driving duties. She thanked the Reverend Mother for her help and made her way back to her car.

It only took her just over half an hour to drive into Hexham and park her car outside a large supermarket, which was new since her days of living locally.

The market was still there, though, she discovered a little later when the majority of her shopping was done. She wandered round it, and gave in to the temptation to buy several different portions of cheese from a farm produce stall. There were also fresh local vegetables, which looked much fresher than those from the supermarket...her aunt had always grown her own, and so could she, provided Marcus's gardener was prepared to help her.

She made her way back to her car, pausing to watch the bustle of the busy Tuesday cattle market. The remains of the abbey basked in the warmth of the sun. It made her feel both sad and elevated to reflect on how many generations of people had lived in this small town.

She didn't rush to drive back, telling herself that she wanted to take in the beauty of the countryside, so long forbidden to her, but it was only when she was within five miles of home and her accelerator needle started to drop still lower that she acknowledged that it was not so much her desire to admire the countryside that was delaying her, but her reluctance to return home.

When she eventually turned into the drive, she discovered that someone else was driving down it ahead of her in a bright red Mini. It stopped neatly in the courtyard, and Maggie parked next to it. A pretty, plump woman in her early forties climbed out. She had dark auburn hair, softly curled and well-styled, her pale green linen separates a perfect foil for her colouring.

As Maggie got out of her own car, the older woman gave her a puzzled look.

'I'm Maggie Deveril,' Maggie told her, introducing herself.

'Oh, yes, of course.' The puzzled look disappeared. 'The photo on Marcus's desk. I thought I recognised you, but... I'm Marcus's secretary,

Anna Barnes.' And, despite Isobel's catty remarks, quite definitely not in love with her boss, Maggie judged shrewdly.

As she extended her hand, Maggie noticed the glint of gold from her wedding finger.

'Since Marcus has had his accident, I've been bringing the post out to him every day so that he can check through it. I did offer to chauffeur him to and from the office, but the pins holding the bones had been giving him a lot of pain, and I don't think he much cares for the idea of being cramped up inside a car.'

'Pins?' Maggie queried, uneasily. The word sounded rather ominous and, although she didn't know much about medical matters, she would not have thought pins necessary for a simple break.

'Well, yes,' Anna Barnes confirmed, looking rather awkward and uncomfortable. 'It was such a bad break. His leg was crushed in several places by the weight of his horse...and yet, do you know, I think Marcus was more concerned for the poor beast than for himself. He was furious with Isobel...really tore a strip off her, I believe, told her she had no right to bring the dog out when it wasn't properly trained.'

Maggie badly needed to sit down. She had been feeling oddly sick ever since Anna had innocently revealed to her just how serious Marcus's accident had been. He might have been killed. He was lucky he had *not* been killed in fact. And if he had been, she would have known nothing about it. A sensation not unlike someone jerking painfully on her heart caused her to tremble violently at the thought of Marcus dying without her being aware of it.

'Oh, heavens, you've gone as white as a sheet,' Anna apologised guiltily. 'I take it you didn't know?'

'Not the details... I just thought he'd taken a tumble.'

'Look, I think we'd better get you inside so that you can sit down,' Anna said gently, firmly taking hold of Maggie's arm.

Maggie gestured vaguely towards the car and her shopping, murmuring something which Anna obviously managed to interpret, because she said soothingly, 'No, we'll leave it there for now. It won't come to any harm,' and somehow or other Maggie found herself inside the cool kitchen and being firmly pushed into one of the wooden armchairs.

'Tell me what happened,' she demanded huskily. 'I had no idea.'

Anna didn't seem to find either her urgency or her shock odd.

'I'll put some coffee on first, shall I? If I know Marcus, he'll be ready for a cup.' She made a face. 'I must say I'm not sorry you're here. Mrs Nesbitt was all right in her way...not my idea of a good housekeeper, but some women are inclined to take advantage of a man living on his own, aren't they? And he never seemed to mind. But once she left... Well, I know it isn't easy taking charge of a house like this, but Marcus pays good wages and he was prepared to get extra help in. It's not paying for staff these days, though, is it? It's finding them. And then there's the extra responsibility of the girls. I've got one of my own and a boy as well, so I know what it's all about...'

'The accident,' Maggie interrupted her, her voice raw... Her throat was dry, speaking a painful necessity. Her eyes burned and felt gritty with the weight of unshed tears. Her stomach was churning like a cement mixer, her whole body ready to shake with shock.

Anna gave her a quick, assessing look.

'He'd gone out riding. Not with Isobel, apparently, but she must have seen him and followed him. Her father spoils her to death, and he bought her one of those toy four-wheel-drive things last year. It's painted red and white. Horrible little thing really, and dangerous too, I'm sure. Anyway she'd got this dog in it—or puppy, really...another present from an old boyfriend, apparently.' She raised her eyebrows. 'Rumour had it at one time...' And then she broke off and added hastily, 'But you know what people are like round here...and anyway, he's dating someone else now.'

'The accident,' Maggie intervened fiercely. She didn't want to hear about Isobel's supposed relationship with anyone else...she wasn't the slightest bit interested in the other woman's love-life. She wanted to know about Marcus. Marcus, who could have died and she would not have known... Or would she? Would she somehow or other have felt the lack of his human form inhabiting the same space of time as her own? Would her instincts have told her...warned her?

'Well, she drove off after him and eventually caught up with him just inside the Howards' four-acre field. Stupid woman that she is, she drove right across his path, and of course his horse took fright, reared up on its back legs... He might have been able to bring it back under control, but the dog leapt out of the car and ran right under the horse's hooves, barking its head off.

'Well, that did it. The horse panicked and reared again. It fell over sideways, taking Marcus with it. And even then that stupid girl Isobel had no more sense than to stand there screaming, but luckily Ted Howard had seen everything. He went back to the house for his gun...'

She gave a comprehensive shrug of her shoulders.

'Marcus was very lucky that they were able to save his leg. He's still in a lot of pain, although he won't admit it. He collapsed shortly after Ted reached him. Concussion!

'I must say, we were all surprised when we learned that he and Isobel were getting engaged. They'd been out together several times, but no one had any idea it was that serious. We all knew she was visiting him in hospital.'

'How long have they been engaged?' Maggie interrupted her.

'Oh, not long. They announced it the day he came home from hospital.' She glanced at her watch and said briskly, 'Look, I'd better go and let Marcus know I've arrived. Will you be all right?'

'I'm fine now,' Maggie told her. 'It was just the shock.' She bit her lip and looked directly at the older woman. 'Look...please don't say anything to Marcus about...'

'About what?' a harsh male voice demanded, and Maggie swung round, appalled to discover Marcus standing in the doorway to the kitchen.

Anna said nothing, but Maggie knew she couldn't ignore the question; for one thing, it wouldn't be fair to the older woman.

'I felt rather faint when I was outside,' she said evasively. 'I didn't want to worry you.'

The dark eyebrows rose steeply, the look in his eyes betraying his disbelief.

'It was my fault, actually,' Anna intervened hastily, obviously aware of the tension building between them. 'I had no idea that Maggie wasn't aware of the seriousness of your accident.' She gave Maggie an apologetic look as she added, 'I'm afraid I gave her rather a shock.'

Maggie couldn't tear her attention away from Marcus's face. She saw disbelief give way to frowning concentration and then thoughtful scrutiny as he looked at her.

'You know how squeamish I've always been,' she told him hastily, and a little untruthfully. 'That stupid imagination of mine...' She plucked nervously at her shirt buttons, unaware of the haunting look of anguish darkening her eyes. 'I couldn't stop myself from visualising...'

She raised her head and looked at him, the words she had been going to say dying on her lips. He seemed to hold her under some kind of hypnotic spell with his gaze, forcing her to surrender to the force of it, forcing her to say huskily, 'You could have been killed, and I wouldn't have known...'

Tears blocked her throat. She could hear them herself in her own voice. Panic took hold of her. What on earth was she saying? What on earth was she doing?

Marcus took a step towards her and then, as the panic and desperation flashed betrayingly through her eyes, he stood still.

'As you just said,' he told her in a flat voice, which seemed, to her too sensitive ears, to hold just a touch of cynicism, 'you always did have far too much imagination.'

He turned round awkwardly, heading for the door. Giving Maggie a sympathetic look, Anna followed him.

How to make a prize fool of yourself in four easy movements, Maggie reflected savagely as she got up. What on earth had possessed her to carry on like that? Of course it had been a shock…but surely she had enough self-possession, enough self-control to… To what? To pretend she didn't care?

The cup she had picked up off the table to take over to the sink slipped through her fingers and crashed to the floor. She stood staring at the broken shreds without really seeing them.

Why did she *need* to pretend? She *didn't* care. *Hadn't* cared for a long, long time. The only reason she had been able to let herself come back was because she *knew* that she didn't care.

She bent to pick up the broken mug, her movements slow and awkward, as though she had suddenly turned into an old woman. Kneeling on the floor, gathering the china, she suddenly stopped what she was doing and pressed her hands to her face as her body shook in silent anguish.

She didn't care. She couldn't care. She must not care. But she did… She always had, and she always would.

CHAPTER SEVEN

LATER, when she was rational enough to care who might have witnessed her self-betrayal, she was glad that Marcus had been fully occupied in his study and that the girls were at school; that way at least she need not fear that anyone else had witnessed the total disintegration which had torn her apart when the truth sank in.

She wasn't yet strong enough to admit whether it was love or hatred she felt for Marcus, but what she could no longer deny was that it was the strongest emotion she had ever experienced in her life. Far too strong an emotion, and as she carefully placed the shards of broken pottery outside in the dustbin her movements were those of an old woman, not one of not quite twenty-eight.

The sun warmed the ancient walls of the house and the rough cobbles of the courtyard, but its heat failed to penetrate through the intense cold which had gripped her.

How could she stay here in the knowledge that she was as still as dangerously capable of focusing her whole life on Marcus now as she had been ten years ago? How could she stay, and yet, how could she not?

She wasn't a teenager any more, but a mature woman with loyalties and responsibilities. She couldn't simply turn and run away any more. There were the girls to think of... Her promise to them that she would stay... Herself to face if she broke that promise. And this time, surely, forewarned was forearmed?

It wasn't going to be as it had been before. Marcus was already engaged. She was not that same child who had misguidedly persuaded herself that he loved her.

Oh, God, why on earth had she come back here? Why on earth had she allowed herself to give in to that crazy need to make atonement...to reach out to her past and bridge the distance between it and her future?

Unless *this* was to be her penance...*this* the payment which would be exacted from her for the past: that she must stand and watch, a silent, anguished witness to Marcus's love for and life with someone else.

She realised she was still standing in the courtyard. She turned her head and the brilliance of the sunshine blinded her. She shaded her eyes instinctively, her hand betraying her agitation with its fine tremor.

Dear heaven, this couldn't be happening, but it

was… While she stood here as motionless as the stone doves on the rim of the drinking fountain, her world had turned full circle around her, leaving her defenceless to the enormity of what had happened.

'Boss said you wanted to have a word about the kitchen garden.'

The Northumberland accent was familiar to her, but the voice wasn't, nor the man who addressed her, shocking her out of the bewilderment and into the realisation that anyone could have walked out of the house and read her unguarded face.

Luckily he had approached her from behind, and before she turned round she managed to compose herself a little.

He was about sixty, with sparse, grizzled grey hair and sharp blue eyes. His skin was burned by years of exposure to sun and wind.

'John Holmes,' he introduced himself. 'I come round a couple of times a week to do the gardens. Not the lawns. My lads do that…but the borders. Fine borders you've got here, planted by…'

'My grandmother,' Maggie supplied for him, pulling herself together.

She saw from the shrewd look he gave her that he knew of her connection with the house. No doubt the entire village knew she was back by now.

In her grandfather's day they had employed a full-time gardener, but he had died some two years

before she left, and after that the gardening had
been done by a local firm of contract gardeners.

'Don't do much myself these days... Rheuma-
tism doesn't allow me. But yon borders, now...'

'They are lovely,' Maggie agreed, and he gave
her another sharp look.

'Lovely they might be, but they takes a lot of
hard work. Borders allus do...'

Maggie remembered being told that her grandmother's perennial borders had been her pride and
joy. Planted against immaculately clipped yew
hedges, either side of a brick path, they stretched
for thirty yards along the front of the house, just
beyond the terrace, and were a blaze of colour all
through the summer months. Her grandmother had
apparently been a keen gardener and had adapted
one of Gertrude Jekyll's plans for a one-colour border.

These at Deveril were all in blues, from the palest
white-blue to the darkest purple of larkspurs and
delphiniums, so tall that their spikes topped the
green backcloth of the hedge against which the borders were planted.

'What is it exactly you've got in mind for the
vegetable garden? A rare sight it is now, choked
with weeds and nettles.'

Maggie tried to concentrate on what he was saying to her.

'Told me to see you about it this morning, did

Mr Marcus. Always likes to walk along the border first thing on a fine summer's morning. Knows a lot about plants, does Mr Marcus.'

Yes, Marcus had always loved that part of the garden. Her heart gave a painful wrench as she remembered the number of times she had sneaked out early to waylay him on his early-morning walk. She would have thought that, in view of his accident, he would have chosen to abandon it for a few months. As she remembered what Anna had told her about his fall, she felt faint again, and put out a hand to touch the comforting warmth of the kitchen wall to steady herself.

'I know the kitchen garden's in a bit of a state,' she agreed when she felt reasonably confident that her voice wouldn't betray her. 'But if it could be cleaned up, I thought we might be able to make some use of it. The girls might find it interesting to grow their own vegetables.'

'Well, if it's just cleaning you want...' He scratched his head. 'I suppose if I put some of my lads on to it, we could have half of it ready for autumn planting... Course, the fruit bushes will have to come out and be replaced...and then it will need manuring...cheaper to buy your veg from the market come market day,' he said warningly. 'Mind you,' he added judiciously, 'can't say as I don't prefer 'em home-grown myself. So we'll have half of it cleared in time for the autumn, and then we should have the rest ready for spring…and if you give me a bit of warning, I dare say my lads will look to your plantings should yon girls not be as interested as you wish. Everyone likes gardening when it's like this,' he added, looking up at the sun. 'But when it's cold and wet… Well, then, that's a different kettle of fish entirely.'

She had yet to meet a gardener who was anything but lugubrious, Maggie reflected tiredly after he had left her. Any other time she would have enjoyed her encounter with him, but this morning she had just not been in the mood. She had far too much on her mind.

When she eventually went inside, she was only half surprised to discover that she was physically shaking. The plans she had made with such optimism only a very short time ago were now as alien to her as though she'd had no part in their formulation at all.

She stared at the groceries she had brought back from the market as though she had never seen them before. What on earth had possessed her to put herself in such danger? Had she honestly thought that she could defy fate? Had she genuinely believed that her feelings for Marcus would disappear like morning mist in the heat of the summer sun?

She shook her head tiredly. Did it really matter now whether it had been folly or ignorance which had brought her here? Here she was, and here she would have to stay. She gave a tiny shudder which had nothing to do with the coolness of the kitchen after the heat of the courtyard. There were things she ought to be doing, but somehow or other she simply couldn't summon the energy to do them. All she really wanted to do was to hide herself away from reality and the rest of the world, and most of all from Marcus's far too sharp eyes.

She had been torn to shreds once on the cruel sharpness of Marcus's too penetrating scrutiny. It might have been ten years ago, but the memory of how he had looked at her then was still sharp enough to bring another shudder to her body.

She couldn't just sit here staring into space, her senses warned her. She must get up; do something. Her attention was caught by the vegetables heaped in the middle of the deal table. There was meat as well—fresh lamb cutlets. She felt rather like someone who had jumped into shallow water, only to discover it was fathoms deep. She had plunged unaware into those shocking, icy depths, and now, slowly and painfully, she was making her way back to the surface. By the time Anna eventually walked back into the kitchen, laden down with bundles of files, the atmosphere was rich with the scent of cooking meat. She sniffed appreciatively and then grimaced, patting her hips.

'Salad for me tonight, unfortunately. When my husband's away on business I try to do a bit of dieting.' She glanced enviously at Maggie's slim figure. 'You don't look as though you've ever had a weight problem,' she commented.

'Not really,' Maggie agreed, not telling her that when she had first gone to London she had been so thin and her appetite so poor that John Philips had threatened to take her himself to the doctor unless she started eating better. It was only years later that she'd realised how close she had come to being a victim of the slimmer's disease, anorexia nervosa.

These days she normally ate sensibly and well, but it didn't take much to make her lose her appetite. Right now, for instance, the very smell of the meat cooking was enough to make her feel quite nauseous.

She was planning to make a lamb casserole delicately flavoured with herbs. It was one which had been a favourite of her uncle's, and was almost one of the first dishes that Marcus's mother had taught her to cook. Her hand trembled slightly as she paused in chopping up herbs.

'You still look rather pale,' Anna commented, looking at her curiously. 'Are you sure you're feeling all right?'

'I'm fine,' Maggie assured her lightly. 'It's just the sun. Last summer the weather was so poor that I suppose we're not used to it.'

'Mmm. Well, let's hope a good meal will have a mellowing effect on Marcus's temper,' Anna commented drily. 'He certainly seems to be in a foul mood at the moment.' She made a face. 'I thought men were supposed to mellow once they got engaged.'

Maggie's hand was shaking so much, she had to put the knife down.

Don't talk to me about Marcus. Don't tell me about his engagement to someone else. It hurts too much, she cried out inside, but of course the words remained unspoken. How could she speak them? How could she do anything other than bend her head and hope that Anna was putting her lack of comment down to the face that she was engrossed in what she was doing.

'Of course, I know he's still suffering a lot of pain,' Anna continued, apparently oblivious to Maggie's rigid back and downbent head. 'And the doctor's already forecasting that there's going to be a certain degree of residual lack of flexibility in the muscles.'

The knife clattered on to the floor, making a sharp noise as Maggie jerked upright. As both women bent to retrieve it, Anna looked directly at her.

'He's going through a very hard time at the moment,' she said quietly. 'Try to be patient with him, won't you? You're what he needs.'

Maggie blenched, the hand holding the knife going bone-white as she fought to resist the emotional impact of what Anna was saying to her. Of course, the other woman had no idea of her real feelings. No idea at all of the torment she was inflicting upon her.

'Isobel might be a glamour-puss, but something tells me she's not exactly a soothing influence on a man when he isn't feeling at his best. She has been spoiled and indulged all her life, and I rather think she's finding it heavy-going having an invalid as a fiancé. Marcus isn't exactly the kind of man who'd dance attendance on a woman at the best of times, and then of course, I suppose it's only natural that both of them must be suffering from a certain degree of sexual frustration,' she said frankly.

Maggie expelled her breath in a small betraying hiss as she fought to control her expression.

'Of course, they haven't actually been living together,' Anna continued, completely obliviously. 'Life being what it is nowadays, I presume that they must already be lovers. I can see that Marcus might have considered holding back in view of his position of responsibility towards the girls, but Isobel now—well...' she told Maggie grimly, 'I doubt very much if that young lady ever waited for anything that she wanted in her life, and I'm quite certain she's never even thought of considering anyone else's feelings or emotions.'

Maggie couldn't say a word. She was being tortured by the shocking clarity with which her mind

PENNY JORDAN   141

was already picturing Marcus and Isobel together embracing as lovers.

'Oh, dear, I'm afraid I'm letting my tongue run away with me,' Anna said ruefully, mistaking her silence for disapproval. 'Please don't misunderstand me. I wasn't gossiping. It's just that I'm very fond of Marcus. I've worked with him for the last five years and I respect him, not just as a boss but as a man as well. In fact,' she added with a rich chuckle, 'if I wasn't so well married to my Peter I think I might be in danger of joining my emancipated sisters and consider the attractions of taking a younger man as a lover. It's been very hard for him, these last few weeks since the accident,' she added in a quieter tone, 'and Isobel hasn't been any help to him at all, apart from nagging him to send the girls off to boarding-school.

'Oh, yes, I know all about that,' she admitted when Maggie looked at her. 'And I must say that I don't believe that it's in their best interests to send them away, not at this stage in their lives. Susie, especially, is very vulnerable at the moment. She's at that age when she might conceivably see being sent away to school as a rejection of her as a person and not simply an expedient means of dealing with a difficult problem.'

'I suppose it's only natural that Isobel should want Marcus to herself once they're married,' Maggie said non-committally.

'Natural, but very selfish. She's always known that Marcus has the responsibility of the girls.' She shifted the weight of the files in her arms and said ruefully, 'I think I've spent enough time gossiping for one day. I'd better get into the car and back to the office.'

She liked Anna and could quite conceivably see the other woman becoming a close friend in time, Maggie acknowledged when she was on her own in the kitchen, but it was very difficult for her to react naturally to the other woman's confidences, even when she knew they were being given for the very best of reasons and out of her concern for Marcus, rather than out of any desire to simply discuss his relationship with Isobel. Even now, long after Anna had gone, she was still feeling sick and shaken by the other woman's disclosure that she believed that Marcus and Isobel were lovers, and yet what on earth had she herself expected? They were both adults, and a sexual relationship, as she knew from living in London, was a natural and totally acceptable part of a relationship between engaged couples these days.

She finished preparing the casserole and put it in the oven at a low heat. It was time to go to collect the girls from school, and she still hadn't made any attempt to get in touch with the people on the list the Reverend Mother had given her to see if she could arrange to share the school run with some of the other parents living locally. It was something she could have asked Marcus about if she had felt strong enough to be able to face him and to behave naturally with him.

After this morning's appalling discovery that she still loved him, the thought uppermost in her mind was that she must keep as much distance between them as possible until such times as she had come to terms with her feelings. She checked that the oven was on an appropriately low setting and walked towards the kitchen door, opening it, hesitating with her hand on the handle. Had the relationship between them been more normal, wouldn't she have popped her head round the study door to let Marcus know where she was going?

She closed her eyes and gave a tiny sigh, too drained to fight the combined depression and tension invading her. How long would it be before she was free of this tormentingly seductive inner voice that coaxed her to throw caution to the winds and to use every logical excuse she could find simply to be with Marcus, but she wasn't here to indulge her own unwanted emotional yearnings. She was here to take care of her two younger cousins.

Resolutely she stepped back inside the kitchen and shut the door firmly. There was no need, after all, to alert Marcus to her departure. He knew she was in the house, and if he wanted to speak to her he was certainly capable of coming to look for her.

On her way to her car, she wondered idly if Isobel worked. The other girl had mentioned helping her father out at the surgery, but presumably this didn't occupy very much of her time.

She opened her car door, grimacing a little at the heat which had built up inside it. Getting in and starting the engine, she wound down the windows and then drove slowly out of the courtyard. On her way past the entrance to the kitchen garden, she heard sounds from inside it which suggested that the gardener had already set his men to work there.

It had been a long time since she had done any gardening. She had always enjoyed planting things and watching them grow. She had also enjoyed the privacy and solitude of the enclosed garden. There had been ample opportunity to daydream when she worked there, tugging the weeds from the rich earth, but she had already endured one very painful lesson about the folly of allowing daydreams to become confused with reality, and there was no way she was going to fall into that same trap again.

She arrived at the school in plenty of time to collect the girls, but their departure was delayed when they insisted on introducing her to some of their friends. A variety of nicknames ran through her brain in a confusing jumble as each girl in the large group was pulled forward and introduced to, 'Our cousin—you know, the one who lives in London and illustrates books.'

Wryly aware that many of the girls who were regarding her now with a mixture of awe and curiosity would be destined to go on to university and from there to careers far more worthwhile than her own, Maggie wondered how long it would be before they ceased to look up at her in awe and rather would tend to look down on her with typical teenage arrogance.

Several older women had joined the group now, mothers mainly of the girls to whom she had already been introduced, and another round of introductions began.

'And this is Alison's Aunt Jane,' Susie introduced, Alison being the friend the two girls had been with when Maggie had arrived. The older woman looked a little confused at the introduction, and Maggie suspected that, like the other women to whom she had been introduced, she had not really known whether Maggie actually existed or was simply a figment of Susie and Sara's joint imaginations.

'I had no idea that Marcus had any family, other than the girls,' she admitted frankly, as she shook Maggie's hand.

'I don't think he has,' Maggie agreed calmly. 'Marcus and I aren't actually related, at least not by blood,' and she gave a brief description of her own antecedents, causing the other woman to comment in some surprise.

'Oh, yes, I seem to remember my husband's pre-
decessor remarking that there was another Deveril.
Charles, my husband, is the vicar,' she added by
way of explanation. 'We've been here about eight
years now, and I must admit I'm dreading the day
coming when we have to leave. My sister and her
husband work abroad, and Alison lives with us during term-time, flying out to them for the longer hol-
idays.' She made a face. 'Not an ideal situation, but
fortunately Alison has a very placid and equable
temperament and she seems to cope very well with
it. I'm just sorry that my own two girls are grown
up and living away from home now, because it does
tend to make things rather lonely for her. At least
Susie and Sara have each other. Is this to be a short
visit, or…?' she asked curiously as Maggie headed
back towards her car.

'I'm to be here permanently. At least until the
girls have finished their schooling,' Maggie told
her, not resenting her questions and knowing that
they sprang from genuine concern for the two girls'
welfare than from any desire to gather the latest
gossip.

'Yes, they're old enough now to need a sympathetic female influence in their lives. Marcus has
done a marvellous of bringing them up, but I think
this accident has brought home to him the fact that
they're now both at an age when they need more

emotional support than any housekeeper, however excellent, can give them.'

She didn't ask any further questions, simply giving Maggie a warm smile as they parted and saying in a friendly voice, 'If you feel like a chat at any time, or if there's anything you need to know that you think I might be able to help with, please don't hesitate to give me a ring or pop round.'

Thanking her, Maggie ushered the two girls into the car and then got into the driving seat. 'Everyone was really surprised at lunch time when we told them about you,' Susie chattered enthusiastically as Maggie headed for home.

'Yes. They thought Susie was just making it up at first when she said you were coming to live with us,' Sara chimed in, and through the driving mirror Maggie just caught the fleeting expression of concern cross the older girl's face, as though even now she was still worried that Maggie might change her mind and go back to London.

How could she? She had given her word, and besides, she was coming to realise that looking after the girls wasn't going to be any sinecure and that they did genuinely need her, as did Marcus, although she had little doubt that he would be very reluctant to admit as much.

Without her to take charge of Susie and Sara, he would be in the very uncomfortable position of either having to give in to Isobel and send them away to boarding-school, or having to refuse Isobel's demands, running the risk of plunging them all into a very unhappy home life indeed. Maggie tried to imagine what Deveril House would be like with Isobel as a new bride, desperately trying to get rid of the two half-sisters-in-law she had absolutely no desire to have living there.

No, that would not have been an ideal situation for two teenage girls at a highly impressionable stage in their lives, when their future emotional development could depend on the atmosphere in which they were living. What would happen when Marcus and Isobel married? Maggie gave a tiny shiver, trying to imagine what it would be like trying to live under the same roof as Marcus and his bride.

It was like a fine torture being applied to already overstretched nerves. Her heartbeat picked up, her pulses racing rapidly as she fought against the nausea rising up to her throat. She couldn't endure it. She knew now that she wouldn't be able to endure it, but Isobel and Marcus weren't getting married almost for another twelve months. Time, surely, for her to get her unwanted feelings under control and for her to come to terms with the fact that Marcus had no role in her life other than as her cousins' half-brother.

As she tried to concentrate on her driving, she told herself grimly that, whatever else she didn't manage to do, she must make sure that Isobel never discovered how she felt about Marcus. Once the other girl knew that, Maggie sensed that she would take great pleasure in making her life as miserable as she could. Not out of resentment or jealousy, but simply because it would amuse her to torment Maggie with Marcus's unavailability, just as she had enjoyed holding the threat of being sent away to boarding-school over the girl's heads.

Once they were back at the house, Maggie sent both girls upstairs to change out of their school uniform while she prepared a light snack. She had learned that they normally had the time from coming home from school until they sat down for their high tea at six o'clock to themselves, followed by two or three hours concentrating on their homework and then another hour or so relaxing before they went to bed.

She had decided, for reasons that she was not prepared to go into even with herself, that it would be as well if all four of them sat down to dinner together. She had ascertained that, if Marcus was eating in, he normally had his evening meal about eight o'clock to eight-thirty, and so, on the basis of this, she had decided that a light snack at around half-past four would keep the girls going until they all had their evening meal.

They greeted this announcement with expressions of pleasure.

'We always used to eat together, but Isobel said she hated having dinner with two grubby school-girls and so Mrs Nesbitt changed everything round.'

'Yes, and if we're not having dinner until half-past eight, that means that we've still got time to go riding or play tennis and do our homework,' Sara chimed in.

'I haven't said anything to Marcus yet,' Maggie warned them. 'He might not approve, and if he doesn't...' As she spoke, she was setting a tray with a pot of tea and some of the scones she had made that afternoon.

'I thought Marcus might appreciate something to eat,' she said lightly to Susie, gesturing towards the tray. 'Why don't you take this in to him?'

She had her back to the window, and at first didn't realise why Susie suddenly said in tones of deep disgust, 'Oh, no,' and then Isobel walked into the kitchen, giving them all a very disdainful look.

She was wearing a tight-fitting linen dress which showed off her curves to perfection, and as she glanced at it Maggie thought wryly that no receptionist's salary had ever paid for that particular garment. It shrieked Knightsbridge, as did all of Isobel's very glossy appearance. She was wearing a heavy, cloying scent which made Sara wrinkle her nose and grimace.

'Still here?' she commented rudely to Maggie. 'I

should have thought you'd have had enough of the country by now.'

Susie, whose cheeks had started to flush the moment Isobel walked into the kitchen, said angrily, 'Maggie's not going back to London. She's going to stay here to look after us.'

In the brief space of time it took Isobel to recover from the shock of Susie's announcement and to swing round and glare at Maggie with open dislike, Maggie realised that Marcus had obviously not conveyed to Isobel the information that she was going to stay.

'Don't be ridiculous,' Isobel said to Susie, her voice suddenly much sharper and shriller. Her mouth hardened as Susie turned away from her, deliberately ignoring her comment.

Half-way towards the kitchen door, Isobel suddenly turned and swung round on one elegant and high heel to say commandingly to Maggie, 'Bring some coffee to the study, would you?'

It was on the tip of Maggie's tongue to refuse, and then, as though she was half expecting her to do so, Isobel added mockingly, 'After all, if you *are* taking over as housekeeper here, it will be one of your duties, won't it?'

As the kitchen door closed behind her, Maggie seethed. Housekeeper, indeed. If Isobel thought for one moment that she was going to be able to order her around, then she was going to have an awful shock coming.

She saw the look Susie and Sara exchanged and, not wanting to make the situation between Isobel and the two girls even worse than it already was, she suggested calmly, 'Once you two have finished eating, why don't you go outside and get some fresh air before you start your homework?'

'You're not going to make coffee for her, are you?' Susie demanded in tones of deep disgust as she saw that Maggie indeed was.

'Isobel is a guest in this house, and moreover she is Marcus's fiancée,' Maggie pointed out, fighting to keep her voice under control and not betray her real feelings. 'I was just making tea for Marcus anyway,' she added soothingly.

'Well, I think she's got a cheek, speaking to you like that,' Susie told her, plainly in no mood to be placated, 'and Marcus would be furious if he knew. He's always telling us that you should be polite to everyone.'

'Mmm, well, I think you'll find that men in love rarely appreciate having the object of that love criticised by others,' Maggie pointed out warningly to her, but Susie wasn't really listening. Instead she was frowning, as though deep in thought.

'You know, I know they're getting married and that they must be in love, but, well they just don't act like people in love, somehow.'

'I don't expect they do in public,' Maggie agreed, shooing both girls out of the kitchen while she poured the coffee.

It wasn't very far from the kitchen to the study, but nevertheless she had to stand outside the door and take a deep breath, counting slowly to ten, before she felt calm enough to knock on it and push it firmly inwards.

Marcus was standing by the window with his back to her. Isobel was standing in front of the fire looking furiously angry, whether at Marcus or at her interruption, Maggie had no way of knowing.

She almost stumbled as she put the tray down, and Marcus wheeled round, concentrating an icy look of dislike on her. Maggie couldn't get out of the room fast enough. She didn't know quite what she had been dreading when she'd hesitated outside the door. Perhaps it had been the thought of finding the engaged couple locked in a passionate embrace that had made her feel sick with dread.

Certainly she had not anticipated the angry tension which had greeted her, and she wondered if Isobel had yet discovered that, when Marcus had made his mind up about something, no amount of sulking or persuasion could get him to change it.

She was just on her way to the kitchen garden to check on the progress that the men had made when Isobel came hurrying out of the house. The other girl came flying towards her, flags of temper flying in her otherwise pale face.

'This is all your fault,' she announced without preamble. 'Until you came back on the scene poking your nose in where it isn't wanted, Marcus was quite happy with the idea of sending the girls off to boarding-school. But now...' She took a deep breath and glared furiously at Maggie. 'Of course I'm not deceived. I know exactly why you're doing this.'

Maggie felt the earth lurch uncomfortably beneath her feet, a horrible faintness washing over her as she felt the blood drain down her body.

Surely Isobel hadn't realised already? How on earth had she betrayed herself? The other woman must be far more perceptive than she realised, unless...unless Marcus himself... She shook like somebody with a palsy.

'After all, you're not exactly in the first flush of youth, are you?' Isobel was sneering, thoroughly confusing her. 'I suppose the idea of coming back here and living off Marcus must have been too tempting to give up. Quite an opportunity those idiotic little fools have handed to you,' she added savagely. 'And if you think for one moment that I'm going to share my home with you or with them...'

'*Your* home?' Maggie interrupted her, filled with a sudden and glorious rush of adrenalin as she realised that Isobel had no idea of her real feelings for Marcus. 'Perhaps I ought to point out to you that this house was left jointly to Susie, Sara and myself by our grandfather.'

Isobel stared at her in silence, an expression of astonishment slowly giving way to one of malice as she purred tauntingly, 'Is that what you really think? If so, I'm afraid you're way off beam. Your grandfather changed his will shortly before he died, leaving everything to Marcus.'

There was no way that Maggie could conceal her shock.

'Of course it's true that the girls have the right to live here until they come of age, but that proviso can hardly apply to you, can it?' Isobel asked with evident pleasure. '*I* know all this because my father was asked to witness your grandfather's will. I remember Daddy commenting at the time that it was probably the only way your grandfather could think of protecting the estate and Susan and Sara, and one could hardly blame him for disinheriting you, after all.'

Disinheriting her. Maggie felt even sicker than she had done before, and not just sick but terribly cold as well, as though a warm garment she had always carried with her had suddenly been ripped away from her. Until that moment she hadn't realised how much it had always meant to her to know that she had a home here, where her family had lived for so many generations.

She didn't question Isobel's knowledge, nor her grandfather's decision, but it hurt none the less to know she had been excluded.

'So you see, this is Marcus's home and not yours, and once he and I are married...'

Maggie couldn't listen to any more. She pushed past the other woman, ignoring her sharp cry of protest, and stumbled her way towards the gate that led into the kitchen garden. Once there, she sank down on to the stone bench just inside the door, shivering and shaking, unable to do anything other than to try to keep at bay the acute feeling of despair welling up inside her.

One part of her brain registered the noise of Isobel's car as she drove off, another the fact that the angling of the sun meant that time was passing, and then at last, when the numbing sensation of shock had worn off, she got clumsily to her feet and headed slowly back to the house.

CHAPTER EIGHT

BY THE time Maggie had returned to the kitchen, her initial instinct, which had been to barge into Marcus's study and demand to know why he had not told her immediately about her grandfather's will, had faded, and in its place had come a complex tangle of emotions and reactions she was trying hard to come to terms with. Over and above the anguish she felt at knowing how Marcus must be laughing at her for her belief that she had every right to live in Deveril House was the knowledge that she had made a promise to Susie and Sara which she had come dangerously close to breaking when Isobel had dropped her bombshell.

Part of her could hardly bear the thought of staying on at the house now that she knew that she had absolutely no legal right to be there, and part of her ached to walk into Marcus's study and tell him outright that, now that she knew exactly what the position was, she wasn't going to spend another night under his roof; and still another part of her, a mature and wise part she had come to heed during her years in London, cautioned her to say nothing which would prejudice her ability to give Susie and Sara the physical support of her presence. After all, this sane voice reminded her, had Marcus felt so inclined, there had been nothing to stop him telling her himself that she had absolutely no right to claim Deveril House as her home. The fact that he had not told her how wrong she was in believing that her grandfather had willed the house to herself and her two cousins prompted her to wonder if in his heart of hearts he was glad of her opportune arrival, and of the fact that it meant he now had a very good reason not to accede to Isobel's demand that he send his two half-sisters away to school.

After all, if he had wanted them to go to boarding-school, surely he would have made such a decision before they started their secondary education?

She had decided that, rather than have dinner in the stiff formality of the dining-room, which she remembered as a large, chilly room on the north-facing side of the house, they would eat instead in the smaller breakfast-room, which looked out on the formal gardens, and which caught the whole warmth of the morning sun. Since the beautifully starched and laundered linen tablecloths which Maggie remembered from Marcus's mother's day were nowhere to be found, she simply decided instead to leave the polished oak table bare.

An impulse during the afternoon had sent her out

into the garden to walk along the border of which
Marcus and his mother were both so very fond, and
she had judiciously removed from it enough sprays
of flowers to make a very pretty table arrangement
without spoiling the border's perfection. Now softly
arranged in a large blue and white jug, they en-
hanced the informal warmth of the pretty room.

At eight o'clock, Maggie left the kitchen and
paused hesitantly outside the study door before
knocking briefly on it.

'Dinner in half an hour,' she told Marcus shortly,
opening the door and then closing it again before
he could make any comment. Then she ran quickly
upstairs, heading for the second floor and the
school-room.

'Dinner in half an hour,' she told both girls, adding, 'How's the homework going?'

'Almost finished,' Susie assured her. 'What are
we having to eat? I'm starving.'

'Casseroled lamb cutlets,' Maggie told them
promptly. 'It's a recipe your mother taught me.'

There was an odd silence, and then Sara asked
her almost shyly, 'Tell us some more about our
mother. What was she really like?'

Seeing the faint hesitancy and uncertainty in both
sets of eyes, Maggie ignored the fact that she herself had intended to get changed before dinner, and
instead pulled up one of the small, straight-backed
chairs and said thoughtfully, 'Well, she was the sort

of person who always seemed to make everywhere feel warmer just because she was there. It's hard to explain really, but when I first came here just after my own parents had died, I hardly knew your mother. She and my uncle hadn't been married all that long then, and I hadn't wanted to come here to live at all, but it was as though your mother knew exactly how I was feeling. She didn't fuss over me or anything like that.' She broke off and then said with a faint sigh, 'She did so very much for me, gave me so much.'

'Is that why you're going to stay here with us?' Susie asked her, propping her chin up on her hands, elbows on the desk as she stared across the table at Maggie. 'Because of what she did for you?'

'Partially,' Maggie agreed, after considering the comment and deciding that there was no harm in letting her cousins know that she felt a debt of gratitude towards their mother. 'And partially because part of me has always wanted to come back here,' she added, not wanting them to think that she was in any way making a martyr of herself in returning to take care of them. 'And I suppose,' she added musingly, 'the fact that I'm not married and don't have any children of my own means that there's a space in my life which you two will probably fill in the same way that I hope to fill a space in yours.'

She wanted them to know that their relationship would be one of mutual give and take, and that they were not in any way to consider themselves a burden to her.

'Why is that?' Susie asked her. 'That you've never got married, I mean?'

'I don't really know,' Maggie fibbed, after she had subdued the sharp flare of pain the question brought. 'I suppose I just never felt I wanted to.'

'Oh, is that why?' Sara interrupted artlessly. 'Susie thought it might be because you had fallen madly in love.'

'Come on, you two, I'm starving,' Susie announced, cutting right across her sister's comments and knocking her own chair over as she stood up, causing it to crash noisily to the floor.

Maggie felt as though the breath was being squeezed out of her lungs. She put a restraining hand on Susie's shoulder and demanded quietly, 'Who did you think I might be madly in love with, Susie?'

'Oh, no one special,' Susie told her airily, 'and it was a long time ago, anyway, when we first found out about you. I thought perhaps you'd run away to London because you were madly in love with someone and Marcus and Grandfather wouldn't let you marry him.'

'But Susie,' Sara protested, 'you...'

'Come on,' Susie exhorted, ignoring her younger sister. 'I've got to go and wash my hands. They're covered in biro. And so are yours,' she pointed out to Sara. 'See you downstairs,' she called out to Maggie, taking hold of Sara's arm and practically dragging her out of the room with her.

She was an idiot to keep imagining everyone knew how she felt about Marcus, Maggie chided herself as she herself went back downstairs. She paused on the first floor and hurried into her own room. The dusky pink silk dress she had intended to wear lay across the bed. She touched the fabric, and then looked at her reflection in the serviceable cotton blouse and skirt she was already wearing.

Why did she suffer from this foolish need to subject herself once again to a pain she already knew was almost unendurable? Marcus wouldn't look any differently at her if she wore silk or rags. Marcus was far too intelligent, far too astute to love a woman simply for the way she looked. As the thought formed, it was followed quickly by another one.

If Marcus was really so astute, how on earth could he have fallen in love with a woman like Isobel, who was so shallow and heartless that she could contemplate sending two teenage girls to a boarding-school they had no desire to attend simply because she did not want the responsibility of them?

She picked up her brush and tugged it impatiently through her hair, brushing it so hard it crackled with electricity and turned to living fire in the dying rays of the sun. In the end she refused to allow herself the vanity of getting changed, simply exchanging her blouse for a nice blue jumper that matched her skirt. A delicate embroidered detail ran from the shoulder to the wrist, but apart from that the sweater was completely plain. Oblivious to the way its softness outlined the gentle curves of her body, Maggie went back downstairs. She found Marcus in the kitchen, looking at the bare table with some perplexity and irritation.

A feeling of pain and confusion swept over her as she watched him. This was the man she loved. She ached to be able to go up to him and put her hand on his arm, to look at him with all that she felt showing plainly in her face and her eyes. She longed to be able to wipe away the bitterness between them, to tell him simply and truthfully how very much she regretted the pain she had once caused him; but most of all she longed for him to turn and smile at her the way he once had done, and once again admit her to that small and privileged circle of those close to him. But that door was barred to her forever, and in her heart of hearts she acknowledged that it was better so, once he was married to Isobel.

'I thought you said we were eating at half-past eight,' he said harshly, interrupting her thought-flow.

'Yes, everything's ready,' she responded, and

then realised what he meant. 'Oh, I thought we'd eat in the breakfast-room.' Hot colour flooded her face at the way he looked at her. 'If you'd like to go to sit down in there,' she suggested uncomfortably, 'I'll bring dinner through.'

It occurred to her as she watched him limp painfully away that he was probably mentally cursing her for making him walk the unnecessary distance between his study and the kitchen. She also wondered worriedly if he ought to be putting quite so much of a strain on his as yet unmended bones. She knew she was fussing, but she ached for the right to be able to fuss over him properly, to insist that he sit down and not work so hard, to insist that he tried to relax so that those deep furrows marking his forehead would go away and the hard lines etched alongside his mouth ease, and, as the thought formed, she wondered a little bleakly how many of those lines she herself had been responsible for.

She had bought some plump Ogen melons while shopping. Their flesh was sweet and juicy, and, scooped out of the halved fruit and mixed with the sharp freshness of raspberries, it would make a refreshing appetiser for such a hot June night.

She saw Marcus's eyebrows lift a little in surprise when she brought in the starter. Mrs Nesbitt and the temporary staff who had followed her had not bothered with the niceties of three-course meals, she suspected.

Her suspicions were confirmed when the girls' eyes rounded with pleasure.

'Melon...my favourite,' Sara murmured rapturously, eyeing her bowl with the appealing greed of the young.

'Mmm, good for my skin as well,' Susie added. 'All that stodge we get at school, I'm lucky not to be covered in spots.'

'Some of the girls take meals prepared at home by their mothers,' Sara told her guilelessly and, hiding a tiny smile, Maggie promised, 'Well, maybe not this week, it will take me a little while to get settled in properly, but in a couple of weeks' time we'll have a talk about it...'

To her astonishment, Marcus cut in harshly, 'Maggie's going to have enough to do without pandering to the pair of you like that. If you want to take your own lunches to school, then I suggest you make them yourselves.'

Seeing that Sara was genuinely hurt and bewildered by his sharpness, and remembering the temper in which Isobel had come hurrying from the study, Maggie wished she had the sort of relationship with Marcus which would allow her to tell him tartly and in private that it was unfair of him to take out his physical frustrations on his two half-sisters. Instead she suggested palliatively, 'Look, why don't I make your lunches for the first month or so, and then you can take over? It will be good practice for you.'

'For when we get married,' Susie intervened mischievously, pulling a face.

'Not at all. Everyone should know how to cook a basic meal, be they male or female,' Maggie countered calmly. 'Just as everyone should know the proper way to iron a shirt or a blouse,' she added drily, looking at the twisted and unironed collar of the blouse Susie was wearing.

They had all finished their melon, and she got up to collect the dishes and go into the kitchen for the main course, but Marcus gestured frowningly to the two girls and told them, 'Susie, Sara…give Maggie a hand with the dishes.'

To Maggie's surprise, as Susie got up she sketched Marcus a brief, cheeky curtsy and teased easily, 'Yes, oh lord and master. Thy will is my command…'

And, far from being annoyed, an answering grin of appreciation tugged at Marcus's mouth, softening it dramatically as he muttered mock-threateningly, 'If it wasn't for these plaster casts and this crutch…'

'You'd what? Take the dishes out to the kitchen yourself?' Susie teased him again, laughing as she picked up her own and his dish and danced tormentingly just out of reach.

After that, the atmosphere seemed far more relaxed, but Maggie herself was too on edge to enjoy it.

She was pleased to see the girls tucking into the delicately flavoured lamb cutlets with greedy enjoyment, although she did have a very bad moment when Sara paused between mouthfuls to say innocently, 'Maggie told us this afternoon that Mum used to make this especially for you, and that it was one of your favourites.'

Maggie kept her head bent over her own plate, totally unable to lift her gaze to look at Marcus as she prayed he could not think that she had made the dish just because he liked it.

She heard Marcus confirming that the delicately flavoured lamb was indeed one of his favourites, but she dared not allow herself to look directly at him, not even when all the plates were clean and she had to get up to go to the kitchen to bring in the ice-cream she had made during the afternoon. Sweetened with honey and served with more of the fresh raspberries, it had a clean, fresh taste that made both Susie and Sara say enthusiastically that it was the best meal they had had for ages.

There was an expectant pause during which both girls looked at Marcus, and Maggie got up awkwardly, pushing back her chair. She had no wish to hear him paying lip-service to good manners by giving her compliments he would rather have withheld, but instead of agreeing with his half-sisters he said only, 'Susie, Sara…you will both help Maggie with the washing up.' And then he got up himself, such a look of agonised tension crossing his face that Maggie ached to go over to him and help him. It was plain that he was in considerable pain, and she had to bite down hard on her bottom lip to prevent her own small gasp of sympathy escaping.

In point of fact, the kitchen was equipped with an excellent dishwasher, but nevertheless the girls helped her to clear the table and tidy the kitchen. While they loaded the machine, she made coffee, using the beans she had bought and grinding them in the blender.

'Mm…gorgeous smell,' Susie said, sniffing enthusiastically.

'It won't be ready for a few minutes, so I'm just going to dash upstairs and have a look at the north-facing rooms on the second floor.'

'Oh, to use for your painting?' Susie asked knowledgeably. 'Well, they're all virtually empty apart from some old furniture.'

She wasn't gone very long. Any of the four large rooms facing north would do admirably, but, before taking one of them over as a studio and work-room, she would have to check with Marcus that he had no objection to her doing so. She must not forget, after all, that this was Marcus's house and not her own. It was amazing what a difference that knowl-

PENNY JORDAN 169

edge made to her thinking, and she wondered uneasily whether, if she had known the truth earlier,
she would have been so insistent in her determination to stay. Then, she had felt that she had right
on her side...that this house was at least in part her
own home. She felt no possessiveness about the
house from a material point of view, and was sen-
sible enough to realise that there could never have
been any way for her to either buy out her cousins'
shares or indeed run such a large property, and nor
had she ever considered that once they were of age
the property could be sold and the proceeds shared
between them. No, the loss she felt was more of an
emotional than a material one: as though a safety
net had been removed from underneath her.

She had always looked on this house as a refuge...as a cornerstone of her life...as a place where
she had an immutable right to be; and to discover
that she was wrong, that she had no more right to
be here, to call this house her home, than any stray
passer-by made her feel acutely uncomfortable...rather like a trespasser, in fact.

When she got back to the kitchen, she was half
tempted to ask Sara or Susie to take Marcus his
coffee.

He had gone straight back to the study after dinner, announcing that he had work do do.

'Can't be going out with Isobel tonight, then,'

Susie commented after he had gone. 'They don't go
out much at all now. I wonder if they've had a row.'

'Marcus's private life is his own affair,' Maggie
told her severely. 'I'll take this coffee to him, and
then I suggest you two make sure you've got all
your homework finished.'

Either Marcus had made the excuse that he had
work to do simply to get away from her, or he was
finding it difficult to concentrate on it, Maggie reflected as she knocked briefly and then opened the
study door and saw that he was standing in front
of the window with his back to her.

He was dressed casually, as he had been ever
since she had arrived, in a short-sleeved, thin cotton
shirt, through which she could see the hard leanness
of his back, and a pair of faded jeans slit up one
side, to accommodate the cumbersome plaster
which encased him.

She cleared her throat nervously, tensing as he
swung round, his eyes chilly with rejection as he
saw her hovering just inside the door.

'Marcus, if you've got a moment to spare, there's
something I'd like to discuss with you.'

She saw his mouth twist in cynical bitterness and
felt her stomach go hollow as she read the message
of contempt in his cold stare.

'You…discuss? This must be a first.'

And she flushed guiltily at the accuracy of the
thrust, remembering how many times in the past she

had gone her own way, deliberately ignoring his advice, and how, when she'd arrived, she had announced that she was going to stay no matter what he chose to say.

'It's about my work,' she told him quietly, putting the tray of coffee down on his desk. 'I was wondering if you would object if I used one of the north-facing rooms on the second floor. I've got a couple of commissions to finish and...'

She broke off at the terse sound he made, lifting her head instinctively so that she couldn't avoid seeing the surprise that drew a frown to his face.

'Why ask me?' he told her brutally. 'Why not just go ahead and move your stuff in there?'

Maggie flushed again and, much as she wanted to lie to him, she knew she couldn't.

'I felt I had to,' she told him painfully. 'You see, I hadn't realised until Isobel told me this afternoon that Grandfather left the house to you.'

His reaction was not at all what she had been expecting. Contempt...derision...even an outright demand that, since she did now know, she leave the house immediately; she had steeled herself for all of those, but to her shock he bit out sharply, 'Isobel told you *that*?'

'Yes,' Maggie confirmed in some bewilderment.

'And now you want to know just how it came about that your grandfather left his place to me, is that it?'

'No!' Maggie denied, openly appalled. 'Of course not.'

He was looking at her with a rather odd expression...something compounded of pain, sadness and a fine irony that brought a lump to her throat, and took her three or four paces towards him before she realised what she was doing and stopped.

'I know I've hardly given you any grounds to think anything other than the worst of me,' she told him huskily. 'But if my grandfather left the house to you, then I know that he must have had sound and just reasons for doing so. No, it isn't that I wanted to talk to you about...it's...'

'It's...what?' he prompted her in a surprisingly soft voice that had her attention focusing on his face and noticing in confusion that his eyes were suddenly darker and warmer...and that the lines hardening his features had softened and that his mouth—normally when he spoke to her a grim line of disapproval—had softened and curled, so that... She caught her breath and found that she could not release it, just as she could not draw her gaze away from the fullness of that sensual lower curve of his lips, wondering dangerously what it would be like to run her tongue-tip along that tempting outline to probe delicately and teasingly at the closed firmness of his mouth until...

'Maggie?'

The sound of her own name, raw and urgent, and

yet muted as though by distance, made her wrench herself off the path of self-destruction she had been travelling down and focus instead on a spot beyond Marcus's shoulder.

'Where are your thoughts, I wonder, when you slip away like that? With your lover?'

He was so dangerously close to the truth that she replied almost violently, 'No! I don't have a lover. I...'

She broke off as he suddenly seemed to lurch forward and stumble, her one instinct to protect him, so that she ran instinctively to his side, supporting him with the weight of her own body as he grabbed hold of the edge of the desk.

Wedged close against him, her head almost tucked into the hollow where his shoulder joined his arm, pressed against the hard angularity of his hip, her hands holding tightly to his chest and back, the moment the crisis was over and he had steadied himself she was so acutely aware of him that, had she not been trapped between the desk and his body, she suspected she might have been the one to faint.

As it was, she was painfully aware of the musky, hot scent of him, intensely disturbing to her own senses. Strange that as a teenager her fantasies had never encompassed this unexpected eroticism which was already having a shocking effect on her own body.

His good arm, which Marcus had stretched out
to save himself, left the desk to which he had clung,
moving so that somehow or other she was caught
between it and the side of his body. As he moved,
she was pressed so tightly against him that the rip-
ple of his chest muscles dragged the fine cotton of
her jumper tautly against her own body, and the
faint discomfort which had followed the betraying
hardening of her nipples became a definite ache.

She glanced down at her own outline instinctively and nervously, unable to stop herself, hot colour stinging her face at what she saw. Her jumper
was a fine summer weight one, and the bra she was
wearing beneath it an even finer silk. Where once
she would have been thrilled and proud of her
body's feminine awareness of him as a man, and
all too eager for Marcus to be aware of it too, now
she was hideously embarrassed and started immediately to pull away from him, only just man-
aging to resist the impulse to cross her arms protectively against her breasts.

But it was already too late for such concealment
because, as she struggled to move away, she realised that Marcus's attention had already focused on
the betraying outline of her breasts, which gave
away all too plainly the fact that she had been
aroused by her proximity to him.

Any hopes she had harboured that he might not
have noticed were dashed as she raised her head

and saw the amused and almost predatory male satisfaction in his eyes. And then, to her astonishment,
as she struggled away from him, he said softly,
'That's a very pretty sweater you're wearing, Maggie. That particular shade of blue always did suit
you.'

She had to say something...to do something to
salvage her battered pride, and so she said the first
thing that came into her head and fibbed uncon-
vincingly, 'Thank you, but I'm afraid it's not very
warm. I feel quite cold.'

She gave a tiny artificial shiver to back up her
fib, but to her chagrin Marcus responded with very
definite amusement, 'Do you think so? Now I, on
the contrary, find it rather...warm in here,' and it
seemed to Maggie that his amused glance lingered
very deliberately on her flushed face. 'No
lover...mm...' she heard him add in a voice that
sounded almost pleased, and as she turned away
from him she could almost have sworn she heard
him say under his breath, 'What a waste.'

Somehow or other she managed to get to the
door, but as the opened it, he called over to her,
'We haven't finished our conversation—remember?' and she was forced to turn round again and
face him. 'You were about to say something about
the fact that had you known the house belongs to
me...'

Desperately gathering her scattered thoughts,

Maggie tried to concentrate. 'Oh, yes. Well, of course, if I had known…I would never have said what I did about it being my right to stay here…' In a choked voice she added, 'It was very forbearing of you not to…not to point out to me just how wrong I was, there and then.'

'Yes, it was, wasn't it?' Marcus agreed with an irony she couldn't miss.

'If it weren't for the promise I've already given the girls that I'll stay, I would leave immediately,' she continued in a stifled voice, and then, seeing the shuttered look in his eyes, she cried out desperately, 'Oh, it's no use. You'll never believe me, whatever I say, will you? You'll never forget what I did, how I lied…' And then, too overwrought to bear any more, she turned and fled from the room, ignoring his command that she stop.

CHAPTER NINE

ONE week slipped by and then another one, and Maggie found herself slipping into a routine. In the afternoons, when her chores were finished, and before she went to collect the girls from school, she went up to the large north-facing room where she had set up her easel.

Oddly, when she bore in mind all the problems which should have prevented her from working, she found her imagination flourishing, perhaps under the stimulus of the views from her window. And, although she admitted that she herself was hardly in a position to judge, it actually seemed to her that the quality of her work had improved as well.

She had been back home for just over six weeks, and in many ways had come to feel as though she had never been away at all, a deceptive feeling and one which she was at great pains to monitor, when Isobel arrived early one morning to take Marcus into Carlisle where he was having the heavy plaster removed from his leg and its progress checked.

It was mid-afternoon before they returned. Maggie heard them before she saw them, the slam of

Isobel's car reaching her through her open window. With a faint sigh she put down her brushes and went downstairs. Isobel was no housewife, and would be no doubt expecting Maggie to appear and produce coffee and something to eat.

The study door was open as Maggie walked past it, and even if it hadn't been it would have been difficult for her not to hear the raised voices coming from the room: Isobel's shrill and piercing; Marcus's deeper but every bit as angry. Maggie had just drawn level with the door when Isobel came shooting out, her face flushed with rage, her eyes glittering with venom as she glared furiously at Maggie.

'This is all your fault,' she hissed furiously at her as she swept past her. 'If you hadn't insisted on staying here to look after those blasted brats... Well, if Marcus thinks I'm going to marry a man who puts his family before his wife...'

Before Maggie could say a word, she stormed past her, slamming doors behind her and then starting the engine of her car with a lot of unnecessary revving. Biting her lip, Maggie walked past the study and into the kitchen. Isobel was a very volatile woman, it didn't need much intelligence to see that, but Marcus had always been very even-tempered. Still, being in love tended to arouse intense passion in the calmest breast.

She bit her lip harder as she tried to quell the

misery that thinking of Marcus loving Isobel always brought her, and then stood indecisively in the kitchen, torn between wanting to go and ask Marcus how successful the removal of the plaster had been, and feeling that it would be unwise to intrude upon him until he had calmed down from his argument with Isobel. In the end she gave way to caution and went upstairs to collect her raincoat before hurrying out to her car.

The day had been overcast and dull, with the threat of thunder rumbling ominously in the distance. She had some shopping to do before she collected the girls from school, and it was only when she was half-way to Hexham that she realised that, although she had picked up her raincoat, she had forgotten her umbrella. It was the heavy thud of large drops of rain against her windscreen that brought this realisation, and as she drove into Hexham and parked her car she realised that she had overtaken the thunderstorm. With any luck she would have finished her shopping before it reached the town. However, luck, it seemed, was against her, for as she queued up at one of the market stalls to pay for her purchases the sky became ominously dark and, long before the stall-keeper had taken her money and handed her purchases to her, heavy drops of rain were beginning to spatter against the cobbles.

Blinding sheets of lightning rent the sky and

thunder clapped sharply overhead. Maggie had
never been frightened of thunderstorms, but the
idea of getting soaked in the almost torrential rain-
fall now turning the narrow cobbled street into
something approaching a small stream was not an
appealing one. A hotel on the corner of the street,
facing into the square she had just left, caught her
eye. The last time she had visited Hexham, it had
been hot and sunny and lunchers had been sitting
at tables outside watching the busy ebb and flow of
people through the square.

Now the tables were deserted, the umbrellas
closed, and Maggie remembered one of the diners
saying that the small hotel had a very attractive coffee lounge, much favoured by locals and tourists
alike. It would probably be wise for her to shelter
in there until the heaviness of the rain had abated,
and a hot, fresh cup of coffee wouldn't come amiss
either, she reflected, ducking her head and grimacing as she had to almost paddle across the cobbled streets to reach the entrance to the hotel.

Inside, someone had carefully exposed and
cleaned the ancient beams. Despite the fact it was
late July, a log fire was burning cheerfully in the
huge grate. A waitress, carrying a heavy tray of
glasses, shook her head regretfully when Maggie
asked the direction of the coffee-lounge.

'It's only open market days and Saturdays,' she
explained, 'but if you don't mind sitting here I

could bring you a tray of coffee and something to eat.'

Thanking her, Maggie looked round for an empty table. There was only one free in one of the half-dozen or so small alcoves along one wall. It was shadowy, almost dark at this end of the room, and the booths themselves were curtained off from one another, giving them an air of shadowy mystery and privacy.

A man and a woman were sitting in the booth next to her own, and all Maggie could see of them as she removed her raincoat and sat down was their legs, as the light from the lamp on the table illuminated them. The woman was wearing impossibly high heels of the type that Isobel favoured, the man, pale grey leather loafers almost exactly the same shade as the immaculately creased pastel-grey trousers that looked so out of place in this sturdy building, whose customers were mostly burly farmers and their families.

These two had obviously not come in to shelter from the rain, Maggie observed as the smiling waitress reappeared and took her order. There were no signs of damp on either the spindly-heeled court shoes or the soft loafers. Neither were the pale grey trousers marked by rain spots. Idly wondering who this couple were and deciding that they must be tourists, although rather inadequately shod ones if they planned to go round the remains of the abbey,

Maggie was just about to take a sip from the deliciously fragrant coffee the waitress had brought her when she heard Isobel's familiar voice.

She froze instantly, imagining she must be mistaken, half making to get up in her seat, only to subside again as she heard Isobel demanding theatrically, 'Oh, hell, Paul, tell me what I ought to do.'

'You know what you must do,' her companion answered her. His voice wasn't as deep or as attractive as Marcus's, and Maggie felt a faint frisson of distaste run through her, although why, she could not have said. Perhaps it had something to do with the man's immaculate clothes, so plainly out of place in this country setting.

'We can't keep meeting like this,' Isobel interrupted him in some agitation. 'Someone is bound to see us.'

'Does it matter?' the man responded, his voice amused and caressing. 'Let's go back to my place,' Maggie heard him adding softly. 'No one would see us there, and I'd be able to…' His voice dropped lower, but not so low that Maggie couldn't hear quite plainly the intimate and extremely explicit suggestions he was making.

Her face burned, more with indignation on Marcus's behalf than with any shock at what she was overhearing. She waited for Isobel to chide the man and remind him that she was engaged to someone else, but to her astonishment Isobel merely giggled. From the sounds she could hear, Maggie guessed that the pair of them were preparing to leave.

What she did next was something she would come to regret bitterly, but at the time the only thought in her mind was that somehow or other she must protect Marcus's interests. Somehow she must prevent a second engagement from being wrecked, and as she stood up and confronted the departing couple, barring their way, it was with a confused belief etched very firmly in her mind that fate had decided she was to make atonement for her past sins, by being instrumental in preventing Marcus's second chance of happiness from slipping away from him.

Isobel went white when she saw her, grabbing hold of the arm of her companion. He wasn't much taller than Isobel herself, a neat, languid figure with blond hair and a too-white smile that somehow never quite reached his eyes. Compared with Marcus he was nothing, and Maggie couldn't imagine what on earth it was that Isobel could possibly see in him.

'Come on, Paul. Get me out of here, for heaven's sake,' Isobel cried out, and when Maggie reached out to try and stop her she pushed past her, almost causing her to overbalance.

Sick with the implications of what she had witnessed, Maggie sank back into her own seat. She desperately wanted another cup of coffee, but her hand shook so much when she poured it that more of it seemed to end up in the saucer than in the cup. Her mind was a jumble of confused thoughts.

What exactly was Isobel's relationship with Paul, apart from the obvious? The obvious being that they were quite definitely lovers. Maggie winced at the thought. Had Isobel met Paul after she had become engaged to Marcus, or was he perhaps a married man with whom she had had a long-standing affair, or…and then abruptly she remembered Anna Barnes telling her that Isobel had been very heavily involved with another man before she became engaged to Marcus, and that this man had supposedly dumped her in favour of somebody else. She tried to remember what Anna had told her about Isobel's previous boyfriend and could remember nothing. She glanced up uncertainly and saw that the sky was lightening. If she delayed much longer, she would be late collecting the girls.

Finishing her coffee, she picked up her parcels and stood up, and was amazed to find that she was still trembling. It was no business of hers if Isobel chose to have coffee with someone, she tried to tell herself as she headed back to her car, bitterly regretting that she had ever gone into the hotel in the first place. But she had, and now she was the possessor of information she would much rather not have had.

There was absolutely no way she could tell Marcus what she had overheard, but neither was there any way she could conveniently put it out of her mind. Her heart ached for Marcus. He deserved better than Isobel, much, much better, but it was not her place to tell him so.

All the way home Maggie worried about what she had seen and overheard, and, as though the girls too picked up on her introspective mood, they sat quietly in the back of the car. Almost the first thing Maggie saw as she turned into the courtyard was Isobel's car parked next to the door.

As she switched off her engine, she realised the Isobel had only just reached the house ahead of her. Quickly she wondered if her delay had been caused by the fulfilment of the hot desire she had seen burning in Isobel's eyes just before they'd focused on her and she'd realised that she and her lover had been overheard.

The girls went ahead of her into the kitchen, leaving Maggie and Isobel alone.

'I suppose you can't wait to tell Marcus, can you?' Isobel challenged her recklessly, her eyes glittering with malice. 'Well, I'm sorry to deprive you of the opportunity to play Miss Goody Two Shoes, but I'm going to tell him myself.'

Maggie recoiled in disbelief and distress as she

caught the very obvious scent of alcohol on Isobel's breath. Surely the other woman had more sense than to drive when she had been drinking? She was wearing a vibrant dark red lipstick, far too sophisticated and glossy for the country.

'Such a perfect little woman, aren't you?' Isobel hissed venomously at her, and then disappeared into the kitchen before Maggie could defend herself against her malicious remarks.

Both girls had gone upstairs to get changed, and when they came down again Susie reminded her that she had promised to take them down to the vicarage so that they could play tennis with Alison and another friend. All the time they were eating the light snack she had prepared for them, Maggie was tensely aware of Isobel's presence in the study.

What was she saying to Marcus? Was she telling him the truth—that she had spent the afternoon with another man, another lover? Maggie shuddered, trying to put herself in Marcus's place, trying to imagine how she would feel if she had to learn that the person she loved had betrayed her with someone else.

A very thick wall, a corridor and two doors separated the study from the kitchen, and therefore it was not really surprising that no voices, raised or otherwise, should penetrate into the kitchen. The girls were waiting impatiently for her to drive them down to the vicarage.

She had an odd impulse to go into the study to check that everything was all right, but she quelled it, reminding herself that it was not her place to interfere. Nevertheless, after she had dropped the girls off and tactfully refused Mrs Simmonds' offer of a cup of tea, she found she was driving a little faster on the way back then her usual speed.

Just as she was about to turn off the main road into the drive, Isobel's car shot out ahead of her, the tyres squealing protestingly as Isobel turned on to the main road far too quickly and then drove away at a high speed. Her stomach knotted with tension, Maggie drove into the courtyard and parked the car. Her mouth was dry when she went into the kitchen.

She told herself that it was no business of hers what had happened, and yet, as she walked down the corridor past the open study door, she found she was hesitating beside it, lingering there.

'Isobel...' Marcus called out sharply from inside the room, and she had a craven desire to turn and run, but instead she said shakily,

'No, Marcus, it's me...Maggie.' And somehow or other she found that she was inside the room and unable to tear her appalled gaze away from the diamond ring glittering malevolently on top of Marcus's desk. Unable to hold the words back, she swallowed nervously and said huskily, 'Oh, Marcus. I'm so sorry.'

'For me?' He laughed harshly in disbelief. 'Don't give me that, Maggie. Isobel's already passed on your views on our engagement.'

Maggie stared at him, appalled. As far as she could remember, she had said nothing to Isobel that might indicate her true feelings. Surely Isobel hadn't realised how she felt about him?

All the breath seemed to be squeezed out of her lungs. She stared at Marcus like someone in a trance, while her mouth went dry and she had to touch her tongue-tip to her lips to moisten them.

'No denial?' Marcus asked her in a hard voice.

'I...'

'You what, Maggie? You *didn't* tell Isobel how much you pitied her, tied to a man who at best could never be completely free of a limp and who at worst could turn out to be a complete cripple. *Is* that how you see me?' he demanded threateningly, coming across the room towards her and making the air between them almost vibrate with the intensity of his rage. 'As something far less than a whole man who can only excite pity in a woman, and not desire?'

Maggie was horrified. 'No...' she denied. 'No, Marcus! You can't believe I said anything like that!'

'Why not?' he demanded brutally. 'After all, it wouldn't be the first time you've lied about me, would it? Only this time, Maggie, I'm going to teach you a lesson I swear you'll never forget.'

As he grabbed hold of her, Maggie protested desperately, 'No, Marcus. Please... I swear to you, I said nothing to Isobel. Look, I know how much it must hurt you to lose her...'

'You don't know the first thing about what makes me hurt,' he told her, the harsh impact of the words almost bruising the sensitive flesh of her ear. '*You* make me hurt, Maggie,' he told her. 'You make me hurt in ways...'

His right hand, free of the plaster which had encumbered his movements, slid along her throat, his thumb probing the nervous tremor that ridged it as she swallowed. He was looking at her in a way that made her muscles lock in disbelief.

That couldn't really be desire she could see burning in his eyes, turning his face hard and making the colour burn up under his tanned skin, and yet, when she allowed her disbelief to show in her own eyes, he said rawly, 'You see, Maggie, the accident might have smashed virtually every bone in my leg, but it hasn't destroyed my ability to feel, to desire...nor to lie awake at night aching with it, wanting...'

His teeth snapped together, biting off the words, and Maggie tried to wrench away from him.

'It's Isobel you want...not me,' she protested

chokily, adding, 'Marcus, this is madness. You must let me go.'

She could probably have fought her way free of him, but if she did, she could potentially do untold damage to the fragile bones that were not yet healed and which, now free of their supporting plaster, must surely be far too vulnerable to expose to any kind of force.

He saw her looking at him and laughed savagely. 'Go ahead and kick it,' he suggested watching her. 'Go ahead and bring me down, Maggie, the way you've brought me down many, many times before.'

She looked at him, her expression tortured. 'Marcus, you know I can't.'

'No?'

His thumb stroked the fluttering pulse in her throat as though unable to resist the temptation to torment it.

She made a despairing sound of protest and tried to reason with him.

'Marcus, I know you must blame me for what's happened with Isobel. I *know* how you must be feeling, but you can't honestly want to...'

'To what?' he taunted her. 'To take you and strip the clothes from you and then to taste and touch every delectable inch of your far too enticing body?'

She shivered as the words rolled easily off his

tongue, almost with amused detachment, hardly able to credit what she was hearing.

'I can assure you that I do, and indeed have done for longer than I care to think about. I wasn't totally oblivious to all those provocative little messages you used to send me, you know, but in those days I was idiotic enough to believe...'

He broke off and Maggie pleased huskily, 'Marcus, please... I know you're angry with me, but this is all wrong. I don't want you, and...'

She didn't get any further. He looked at her and she could almost see the triumph glittering in his eyes.

'Don't you? That wasn't the message I was getting the other night.'

For a moment she didn't realise what he meant, and then, as his gaze dropped slowly and mockingly to her breasts, she did, and her skin burned.

'That was because I was cold,' she told him defensively. 'I told you at the time.'

'Yes, you told me,' he agreed mockingly. 'But both of us knew you were lying. However, if you'd prefer me to prove it to you...'

She was wearing a simple cotton dress, fitted at the waist, short-sleeved, with a pleated skirt and buttons all the way down the front, and before she could stop him, holding her easily with his left hand, Marcus deftly flicked open the buttons, revealing the creamy paleness of her skin right down to her waist.

'Marcus…no,' Maggie breathed, knowing even as she spoke that she was fighting a losing battle, not so much against him but against herself. Once he touched her…once she felt the warmth of his hands against her flesh…his mouth… She shuddered, deeply frightened by the depth of her craving to be part of him…frightened by her inability to hold on to sanity and remember just why he was doing this.

Another plea of protest whimpered in her throat, but Marcus wasn't listening to her. All his attention was concentrated on the exposed V of flesh revealed as he pushed aside the unfastened bodice of her dress to reveal the swelling softness of her breasts concealed only by the flimsy lace structure of her bra.

He made a sound deep in his throat and goosepimples rose up under her skin, her nipples instantly hardening.

What a betraying reaction, and he hadn't even touched her, Maggie acknowledged weakly. When he did…

When he did, his hands were so gentle that she almost cried out at the tenderness of his touch. As his fingers drew gently on the hard buds of flesh, her spine arched like a bow, all thought of resistance draining from her as her body burst into flames at his touch.

She forgot where they were…or why they were there. She forgot what time it was, what day it was, everything bar the fact that she was actually here at the place she had yearned to be so desperately for so long, at last within the magic circle of Marcus's desire.

His mouth grazed the slender arch of her throat, one hand hard and flat against her spine, supporting her, while his other hand tormented the aching peak of her breast, her senses screaming silently for him to free it from the prison of her bra and to place his mouth against its swollen heat and suck it until he had drawn away completely the frenzied, burning need that rolled inside her.

But oddly, when he did what she had yearned for him to do, she discovered that the fierce movement of his mouth against her flesh increased her desire rather than caused it to abate, and not just increased it, but spread it until there was not a part of her body that didn't ache and throb so violently that she could scarcely draw breath without setting off destructive tremors of sensation.

She touched her own mouth to Marcus's throat, feeling the flesh burn and jump. Her nails scored fiercely against his skin as he released her breast and held her against his body until the sensation of her hard nipples pressed against his bare flesh made him shudder wildly and cover her mouth with his own.

She must have unfastened his shirt, Maggie realised dizzily as he took her hands and pushed them, palms flat, against his torso. While she touched the hard, golden flesh, he shrugged out of his shirt, and she watched him easing himself slightly away from her, trembling from head to foot, caught fast in the toils of sensations so intense that her slender body could scarcely contain them.

'Maggie,' Marcus muttered thickly, reaching for her and moaning something in her ear far more shocking than anything she had overheard between Isobel and Paul. But she was beyond being shocked by what he said, beyond anything other than glorying in her body's total response to him, responding to his verbal torment by pressing herself against him and feeling him shudder deeply. His hands slid inside her dress, skimming her hips and then grasping the round softness of her bottom, kneading the flesh so urgently that her whole body quickened.

She bit frantically at his skin, feeling his muscles flex, feeling the male hardness of him against her as he moved her legs so that he could push one of his between them.

Heat rose up inside her, the fantasies of her teenage years forgotten as she responded frantically to his touch, her teeth biting eagerly at his skin, while her mouth trembled betrayingly against it. The hardness of him, so tantalisingly close to her own flesh and yet so frustratingly far away from the place where she most wanted it to be, made her moan deep in her throat, her body writhing help-lessly against him.

'Tell me you want me,' he demanded harshly against her ear, encouraging the wanton movement of her hips with his hands, hands that spanned and cupped the soft round shape of her, and yet some-how at the same time contrived to torment her with brief, far more intimate caresses that she ached to prolong.

'Tell me,' he demanded again, his voice raw and uneven, and his hand moved, sliding inside her briefs to touch her where her quivering flesh had been yearning for him for what seemed like a life-time.

Maggie moaned, incapable of saying a word as her body pulsed and expanded, trembling on the threshold of a pleasure that beckoned like a mirage, and like a mirage vanished when Marcus removed his hand.

Shivering and suddenly shockingly aware of what she was doing, Maggie tried to pull away from him, protesting, 'No, Marcus... Not now, not here...'

Instead of letting her go, he gripped her arms

savagely, his face contorted and suddenly unfamiliar.

'Yes,' he told her thickly. 'Yes, Maggie. Yes…right here and right now. Like this.' And as he pushed her back against the desk she heard the metallic sound of his zip being unfastened, and in the brief seconds of panic that followed, she had time only to moan a short protest before she felt him lifting her, holding her and then filling her with strong, determined thrusts that blasted from her mind everything bar the frantic, urgent ache that was buried somewhere deep inside her, and the knowledge that she must help him find and ease if she had to die to do so.

The pain, so sharp and so unexpected in the midst of so much frantic pleasure, made her tense and open her eyes in shock, to find Marcus looking back at her, not just in shock but in disbelief and something else, something tinged with pleasure and regret. But before she could question it his body surged against her, and as he fought to control it and ease away from her the pain died and the need grew, and instead of releasing him she clung, whimpering her protests into his throat, her body arching so provocatively and pleadingly against him that he tensed and then covered her mouth with his own to silence the small sounds she was making, his body driving so fiercely into hers that she convulsed with pleasure at each stroke, causing him to cry out sharply, unable to hold back on his own need.

What seemed like a long time after the first strong, convulsive spasms of pleasure had passed, Maggie could still find tiny shudders of after pleasure rippling through her, causing her to shiver openly as Marcus looked down at her broodingly.

'I had no idea that there hadn't been anyone else,' he told her flatly, withdrawing from her and turned his back on her as he struggled with his jeans.

In a state that approached complete mental and physical exhaustion, Maggie made no attempt to redress herself. She tried to move, wincing at the soreness in her muscles, and Marcus swung round to look at her.

As he moved, Maggie looked away, and then she saw Isobel's engagement ring glittering malevolently on the desk, and all at once the realisation of what she had done hit her.

She started to shake violently, and felt Marcus reach out to touch her, but she shrugged him off as though his touch contaminated her.

'Maggie, we *have* to talk...'

'No,' she told him shrilly. 'There's nothing to talk about. You've had your revenge, Marcus. Paid me back for what I did to you. Made me...' She couldn't speak for the tears thickening her voice, but when Marcus made to reach out to her a second time, she swung round violently, shaking her head.

'No…don't touch me. Don't ever touch me again,' she cried out, wrenching away from him.

'Maggie…wait…you don't understand!'

Didn't she? Maggie asked herself bitterly. Of course she did, and she was just about to tell him as much when she heard the car and realised that it was probably the girls coming home. Mrs Simmonds had offered to run them back on her way to visit a friend.

'That will be Susie and Sara,' she told Marcus shakily. She couldn't let them see her like this, and as she heard the kitchen door open and the car drive off she pulled away from Marcus and hurried upstairs.

CHAPTER TEN

SOMEWHERE in the distance, Maggie heard the
church clock chime the hour. She moved restlessly
in her bed, wondering savagely why it was that
when she most needed the merciful oblivion of
sleep it chose to elude her.

She had come to bed at ten-thirty, emotionally
exhausted and almost haunted by her mental image
of Marcus's grim face. Twice after dinner he had
told her that he needed to talk to her, but on both
occasions she had been saved from that confrontation by the girls demanding her attention.

The ordeal couldn't be put off for ever, though,
and when it came she would need to have a water-
tight and face-saving excuse for acting as she had.
Why, oh, why was it that her imagination, the cause
of so much pain and anguish in the past, suddenly
now deserted her, leaving her bereft of any logical
reason why she should have allowed Marcus to
make love to her, other than the truth?

She groaned and rolled over, acknowledging that
it was impossible for her to sleep. She doubted that
she would ever be able to wipe her memory clean

of its image of the shock in Marcus's face as she opened her eyes to look at him, her body lethargic and sated by their lovemaking, her brain dulled... She had known then, as she faced that look of grim disbelief, that making love to her as a person had been the last thing he'd wanted to do. She had even thought she had glimpsed a swift dawning of distaste in the darkening of his eyes, but she had looked away, not wanting to see the truth, not wanting to know.

His desire...his need...his love, they were all for Isobel, and she had simply been a...a convenient body and nothing more.

The clock chimed the quarter-hour. Quarter-past one in the morning; she couldn't lie here like this until it was seven o'clock, going over and over what had happened, wondering how on earth she was going to endure living alongside Marcus from now on, and yet knowing at the same time that she could not break her promise to her cousins.

If only she had some sleeping tablets or something...preferably an entire bottleful, she thought grimly, acknowledging as the thought formed that ending her own life was not the answer.

When she had come to bed, Marcus was still up. She had seen his shadow falling across the desk as she passed the study. Now, much as she longed to go downstairs and make herself a hot, milky drink, the thought that Marcus might still be up kept her where she was.

Her bedside lamp was on; the book she had found and been trying to read lay discarded on the bedside table. The more she thought about the comfort of that hot drink, the more she yearned to taste it, and then, just as she had decided to take the risk of running into Marcus, she thought she heard the sound of a door closing downstairs and immediately she tensed.

Her ears, alert for the slightest sound, caught the faint creak of the stairs, so faint that it was impossible to tell if they were caused by footsteps or were simply the grumblings of an old house settling down for the night.

There were no more sounds, and her breath leaked noisily from her lungs. She was just telling herself that she was acting like a fool when her bedroom door opened and Marcus walked in.

He was carrying a tray with two mugs on it, steam and the smell of hot chocolate emanating from them.

As she looked at him in silent dismay, he leaned heavily against the wall, as though the climb up the stairs had tired him. Her bedside lamp showed her quite plainly the lines of worry and grim determination carved into his face.

'I heard you moving about in bed,' he told her emotionlessly. 'We need to talk, Maggie, and you

know it.' He seemed so tired…so drained, that all
her fear of what such a talk might reveal about her
feelings for him left her.

'Yes,' she agreed shakily, adding with a brave
attempt at humour as she looked at the mugs,
'What's this, Marcus? A peace offering?'

'Well, it certainly isn't drugged or laced with
some magical aphrodisiac, if that's what's worrying
you,' he told her grimly.

He walked over to the bed hesitantly, putting the
tray down on the small table and then looking round
for a chair. As he did so, Maggie noticed him mas-
saging the outside of his thigh as though the muscle
was causing him pain.

'I never asked you how you got on at hospital,'
she said in a low voice.

'Well enough. Apparently it's too soon yet to
know how much residual damage there may or may
not be. They tell me I've been very lucky. It could
have meant an amputation.'

Maggie couldn't help it. She shuddered violently,
her eyes immediately registering her feelings.

'I'm sorry,' she stammered when he looked
frowningly at her. She couldn't tell him of that
brief, shocking mental image she had just had of
him trapped beneath the weight of the fallen
horse…of his body shattered and torn.

'That's all right,' he told her grimly. 'As Isobel
told me this afternoon, no man with any feelings

could expect a woman to feel anything but disgusted horror at the thought of...'

'No...no, it's not that at all,' Maggie interrupted him emotionally, reaching out to touch his arm as he abandoned his search for a chair and sat down on her bed instead.

'No?' he queried wryly. 'What was it, then?'

Biting her lip, Maggie turned away from him. How could she tell him the truth? If she had any sense, she would get this interview over with as quickly as possible.

'I'm sorry about your engagement...about Isobel,' she told him quietly.

'I haven't come up here to talk about that.'

She focused on him properly for the first time, and realised on a tiny shock of pain that, beneath his outward calm, he was almost as tense as she was herself.

'Maggie, just what the hell did you mean when you said earlier that I was punishing you?'

She stared at him, dumbfounded; this was the very last question she had expected.

'I...you must know what I mean,' she stammered at last, and when he made no response other than to continue to watch her in a way that made it plain he wasn't going to let the subject drop, she said painfully, looking away from him and focusing on the bedroom window, 'I know you must hate me, Marcus...for what I did...before. It was a terrible thing to do. I can't offer you any excuse other than to say that...' She paused, her mouth dry, wishing she had never started on this path of torture and knowing that Marcus wouldn't allow her to stop now until she had reached the end; and yet perhaps in saying the words, in admitting to him the folly of her youthful feelings, might there not be some form of catharsis that would free her once and for all from her guilt?

It was enough to make her take a deep breath and turn to face him.

'I was very much in love with you, you see...and I thought...or rather, I'd deceived myself into believing that you loved me in return...not as a cousin or an adopted brother, but as a man. When I heard you saying you were getting engaged...' She gave a deep shudder. 'Oh, Marcus, what can I say, other than that I think perhaps I was a little insane in the way that over-emotional and too intense teenage girls sometimes can be. *You* had given me no reason to believe what I did...it was just my own stupid, dangerous imagination. I believed you loved me because I *wanted* to believe it. I know how you must hate me for what I did, how you must have ached to make me suffer as much as you have done yourself, but believe me, I *have* suffered. All these years of guilt...'

She was almost wringing her hands, her body shaking as the words poured from her, her voice raw and so painful to the man listening to her that he actually found he had to swallow as though to relieve a soreness in his own throat.

'I know I deserve to be punished for what I did then...but your engagement to Isobel... Believe me, I had no intention of destroying that. I know I virtually forced my way in here. I know you don't want me to stay...'

'Don't want you to stay? Maggie, there hasn't been a day or a night for the last ten years when I haven't wanted you to come back.'

Maggie stared at him, her whole body frozen with shock.

'What?' she whispered in disbelief through almost numb lips. 'But that's impossible! You told me to leave. You...'

'I lost my temper...my self-control...I couldn't believe what was happening. I never wanted you to leave home like that, Maggie. You were such a child. I went frantic trying to find you. I lived for months tormented by visions of you alone... hurt...too proud to come back. I couldn't sleep or eat for imagining what might happen to you, and your grandfather was too ill for me to leave him.'

'Yes, I know. I saw the notice in the paper. I suppose I did that, didn't I?' she asked miserably. 'Brought on that third stroke?'

'No,' Marcus told her forcefully, and then added

more gently, 'Oh, Maggie, what burdens I've put on your shoulders. No...I never told your grandfather you'd run away. I let him think you were staying at the vicarage until things had calmed down. I told him...' He checked and then added, 'That third stroke was inevitable, I'm afraid. I already knew that. The doctor had warned me just after he had the second one that it was only a matter of time. In fact, he lived rather longer than either I or the specialist had expected. And while we're on the subject, he changed his will because he wanted to protect all of you...not to punish you. He left the house to me, but with the stipulation that it would always be your home. You were so young, Maggie, and Susie and Sara even younger...'

'Yes...I don't mind...about the house, I mean,' she told him quietly. 'It was just the shock of Isobel telling me.'

'She had no right to do that,' Marcus interrupted fiercely. 'No right at all.'

Maggie stared at him. He was talking about his ex-fiancée as though he loathed her.

'You've no idea what torment I went through wanting to come after you to find you and bring you home where you belonged, but I couldn't leave your grandfather. And then I got your letter saying that you were all right, but that you intended to stay in London...that you were never coming home and that you didn't want any further contact with me.'

Maggie sighed. 'John made me write it.'

'John?' He looked at her sharply, a shadow in his eyes that in other circumstances she would have suspected came from jealousy.

'Yes…' Briefly she explained about her friendship with Lara and her father. 'They tried to persuade me to tell them who I was and where I came from, but when I wouldn't, John insisted that I at least write to you. He couldn't believe that you wouldn't be concerned.'

'He was right,' Marcus agreed grimly. 'I was almost out of my mind. A couple of malicious comments and suddenly my whole world seemed to have blown up in my face.'

He saw Maggie's expression and made a harsh sound deep in his throat, catching hold of her upper arms, his hands warm and firm against her delicate skin.

'*No*, Maggie! Not *your* comments… You said before that I had given you no reason to imagine I saw you as anything other than an adopted sister… That isn't true.'

His fingers tightened momentarily on her skin.

'As for my wanting to punish you…' He gave a bitter laugh. 'If anyone should be punished, it's me! You see, Maggie, I *knew* exactly how you felt about me, and sometimes when you looked at me with those huge, hungry eyes of yours, I'd have to fight with myself not to take you in my arms. You were so young...too young. I knew I'd have to give you time to grow up, but once you had...' He broke off and shook his head.

'But that was before I realised what a selfish brute I was becoming. It took someone's rather malicious comment to show me the truth. A woman— who she was it doesn't matter—an older, rather disappointed woman, I suspect, who pointed out to me one day that women who marry very young are seldom content because they've never been allowed to grow up, and that men who marry very young girls have all manner of emotional problems themselves and are often unable to cope when their child-brides turn into adult women. All generalisations, of course, but her comments held enough of the truth to make me sit back and think about what I was doing to you, about what the kind of life you led was doing to you, and I saw that in all fairness you had to have the opportunity to go out and make your own life...to find out if your feelings for me were those of a child or a woman.

'I lied when I said I was getting engaged, Maggie, but the situation between us was becoming so explosive that it was the only way I could think of to put a distance between us. You were just about to start at college. Your grandfather knew how I felt about you. In fact, he fully approved of the idea of us getting married, but I explained to him that I felt you needed time. But that I knew if I tried to explain to you, you'd probably overrule both my arguments and my common sense. I wanted you so damnably, you see,' he said in a strained voice. 'Ached for you...yearned for you...craved for you; I couldn't trust myself to hold you at arm's length, once either of us crossed that very narrow chasm between us. But everything blew up in my face when you turned on me. I'd underestimated the intensity of your feelings, not made allowances for your intuitive knowledge of how I felt about you...'

'You loved me?' Maggie broke in, stunned by his disclosures. 'You loved me, and yet...'

She broke off, suddenly seeing the wisdom and common sense of what he had tried to do. At seventeen, she had been far too immature for marriage. She had known far too little of human nature, including her own; the age gap between them would have meant that she would have entered marriage not as an adult but as a child, and that such a marriage would ultimately have foundered, she had little doubt at all.

She was not the girl she had been at seventeen: ready to absorb Marcus's opinions as her own because they were his, ready to adore and worship.

And yet, even so, she stared at him with hugely shadowed and pained eyes, asking, 'But why didn't you tell me? Why did you let me go on thinking..?'

'How could I tell you? I haven't seen you in ten years. You have always had the option to come to

me, Maggie… I have never had that same option.
You knew where I was, but you took damn good
care to make sure I could never contact you, and
because of that I assumed that whatever you had
once felt for me had gone and was unregret-
ted…that your life was happy and fulfilled. I
waited…'

'And then one day you decided you were tired
of waiting and got engaged to Isobel,' Maggie supplied wearily for him, but to her surprise he shook
her almost fiercely and denied it.

'No!'

'No? But…'

'Let me tell you about Isobel,' he interrupted her
grimly. 'All her life she's been spoiled rotten. Until
very recently, she had been living in London with
someone. They quarrelled and she came home. He
followed her up here, but Isobel had decided she
wanted to get married. He's very wealthy, you see,
and Isobel had realised she wasn't getting any
younger. He, I suspect, did not share her desire for
married life. She attached herself to me…quite
without encouragement, I assure you. I only know
about her desire to get married because she threw
out some pretty broad hints to me that a husband
wouldn't come amiss. She even pointed out to me
that with two young sisters to bring up, I could
probably do with a wife. Since there was only one
woman I had envisaged in that role, I promptly dis-

abused her of any notion she might have of being that wife, or at least I thought I had until I came round in hospital after the accident and discovered that Isobel and I were engaged, and that moreover, almost the whole county knew about it...'

'So you never asked her to marry you.'

Marcus gave her a grim look and said, 'Do I really look that much of a fool?' He paused and then looked directly at her. 'And then, as though matters weren't already complicated enough, you came back and soon made it very clear indeed that any dreams I had been cherishing that you might have missed me as much as I had done you were just exactly that. But ten years is a long time to go on loving someone, and those kind of dreams can't be abandoned at will.' He gave a rather mirthless smile.

'Before you arrived I had been searching frantically for a way to get rid of Isobel. The only thing I would come up with was to insist that she would have to take charge of the girls. Selfish as she is, I knew she'd balk at the idea of being tied down to this house and two teenagers. And then you came along and bang went my one means of getting Isobel to break off the engagement, or so I thought. I knew there was no way I could allow Isobel to go on imagining we were going to get married. I decided to be honest with her and tell her the truth. You can imagine the shock I got when she barged into my study and announced that she was going back to Paul and that our engagement was off. She seemed to think for some reason that the news wouldn't come as all that much of a shock. Something about you seeing her with him and rushing back here to tell tales...'

'I did see them,' Maggie agreed. 'But I wasn't going to tell you. I couldn't, you see. I couldn't bear the thought of being responsible for breaking a second engagement. I could only think of how much you hated me...'

'Some hatred,' Marcus broke in drily, and Maggie flushed at the look he gave her.

'I thought it was sexual frustration because you and Isobel...your accident...'

He threw back his head and laughed. 'Dear heaven, you'll never know how thankful I was for that accident! The thought of making love to Isobel was a total turn-off, and once you'd come back... Just to set the record straight, Isobel and I have never been lovers, but yes, I was frustrated. Frustrated by years of wanting someone I thought I could never have...frustrated by the sight of that someone here in my home and even more alluring and desirable to me in the flesh than she had been in my dreams...frustrated by my need to break through that wall she had built between us...and most of all, frustrated by the instincts that told me that, no matter what you said, there was something still there between us, some spark that, given the chance, I might possibly be able to turn into a flame that would burn as hotly inside you as my love for you burns within me. Was I right, Maggie? Is there a chance?' he began softly, but she pulled away from him nervously, causing him to check and withdraw, his eyes shockingly bleak before he veiled them from her and looked the other way.

'You're not just saying this because…because of this afternoon, are you?' she blurted out awkwardly. 'I mean, because you discovered that I hadn't had any other lovers? That wasn't just because of how I feel about you, Marcus,' she told him earnestly, not realising what she was betraying, not seeing the sudden gleam that lightened the sombreness of his eyes. 'There's no need to feel you have to…to say that you care about me when you don't.'

'No need at all,' he agreed coolly, and her heart sank. 'In fact, I should have thought that at your age you'd be pretty glad for someone to come along and…'

He turned round just as she was about to explode with angry indignation, and her breath caught in her throat as she saw the laughter and the love in his eyes.

'Idiot,' he told her fondly, pulling her gently towards him, and somehow it seemed quite natural that she should lean her head against him, so that he could hold her comfortably within the curve of his arm.

'I'm sorry if I was rough with you, though. To be honest, by the time things got to the point where I should perhaps have been questioning the wisdom of what I was doing, I was way past any rational thinking.

'As it was, I could scarcely believe that after so many years there you were at last, every bit as warm and welcoming as I'd dreamed...all the woman any man could ever want...and certainly all the woman...the only woman I've ever wanted. Twelve years is a long time for a man to go without a woman, and...'

'Twelve years?' Maggie shot upright in his arms. 'Marcus...'

'I love you,' he told her simply. 'It had to be either you or no one.'

Tears blurred her eyes, and as though he knew what she was feeling he rocked her gently in his arms, his chin resting on top of her silky head.

'Maggie, there's still something you haven't told me.'

She moved and looked up at him and questioned, 'What?'

'How you feel about me. Whether what happened between us was simply a short trip down memory lane, or whether it was the first step forward into a future you want to share with me.'

Maggie looked at him in wonderment. Never in any of her daydreams had she seen him like this: hesitant, uncertain, vulnerable; and her heart flowered with warmth and love.

'I love you, Marcus,' she told him honestly and simply. 'I didn't think I did, not any more, I wouldn't have come home if I'd thought that, and yet perhaps deep down in my subconscious I did know. When I saw you again...that was when I realised that those old feelings had never really gone and that they were still there, a foundation for the love I feel for you today as a woman.'

'My woman,' Marcus told her fiercely, drawing her back into his arms and kissing her with a sharp hunger that made her shake a little with laughter as she acknowledged the vast gulf which had lain between her teenage imaginings and reality.

'What's so funny?' he asked her as he slowly released her.

When she told him, he too grinned. 'I should think so, but if you'd like to make sure...'

THEY DECIDED TO break their news to Susie and Sara over dinner that night. They had agreed that in view of Marcus's 'engagement' to Isobel they would wait three or four months and then get married very quietly, but there was no reason why the girls should not know of their plans.

'There'll probably be a certain degree of gossip,'

Marcus warned her, 'but nothing we can't weather. Isobel's never been particularly popular locally.'

'Oh, I expect there'll be quite a few people who'll think you married me on the rebound,' Maggie agreed, but Marcus shook his head and said with a wicked glint in his smile, 'Not once they see how difficult I find it to keep my hands off you.'

Marcus made the announcement after dinner, as he opened a bottle of vintage champagne.

'There, I told you,' Susie crowed, turning to her sister. 'I told you they'd probably been in love years ago and that that was why Maggie ran away. I knew if we could get her up here, they'd probably fall in love with each other all over again.'

Maggie stared at her, open-mouthed, while Marcus grinned and said to her *sotto voce*, 'Sometimes the power of your sex terrifies me.'

'What on earth made you think that?' Maggie asked Susie.

'Oh, I don't know. I suppose it was the way Marcus looked whenever I asked him about you...and then when you arrived and I saw the way you looked at him, it was easy-peasy after that.' She looked at them thoughtfully, put down her glass of champagne and asked conversationally, 'Marcus, when you and Maggie get married and have children, they'll be our nieces and nephews and our cousins as well, won't they? I hope you have girls, though; I don't like boys...'

Over her head, Marcus looked at Maggie and said drily, 'You will, little sister, you will—and when you do, heaven help them!'

THREE MONTHS LATER Marcus and Maggie married very quietly at the local village church. There was a small reception at the vicarage afterwards, and, watching Susie preening herself in her bridesmaid's outfit in front of the bemused eyes of Marcus's partner's eldest son, Marcus looked at his new wife and said under his breath, 'Does Mrs Simmonds really know what she's doing, offering to take charge of those two while we're away? No, don't go and warn her,' he added as Maggie instinctively looked over her shoulder in the direction of the vicar's wife. 'I've waited twelve years to have you all to myself, and the way I feel right now that's twelve years too long.'

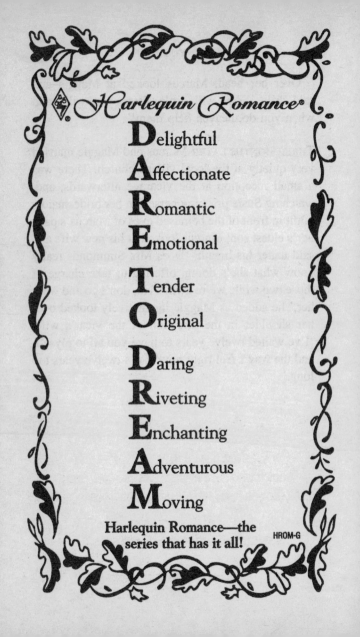

HARLEQUIN ◆ PRESENTS®

**The world's bestselling romance series...
The series that brings you your favorite authors,
month after month:**

Helen Bianchin...Emma Darcy
Lynne Graham...Penny Jordan
Miranda Lee...Sandra Morton
Anne Mather...Carole Mortimer
Susan Napier...Michelle Reid

and many more uniquely talented authors!

Wealthy, powerful, gorgeous men...
Women who have feelings just like your own...
The stories you love, set in exotic, glamorous locations...

HARLEQUIN PRESENTS,
Seduction and passion guaranteed!

Harlequin® Historical

From rugged lawmen and
valiant knights to defiant heiresses
and spirited frontierswomen,
Harlequin Historicals will
capture your imagination with
their dramatic scope, passion
and adventure.

Harlequin Historicals...
they're too good to miss!

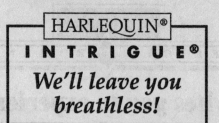

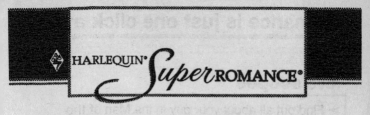

Romance is just one click away!

love scopes

- Find out all about your guy in the Men of the Zodiac area.
- Get your daily horoscope.
- Take a look at our Passionscopes, Lovescopes, Birthday Scopes and more!

join Heart-to-Heart, our interactive community

- Talk with Harlequin authors!
- Meet other readers and chat with other members.
- Join the discussion forums and post messages on our message boards.

romantic ideas

- Get scrumptious meal ideas in the Romantic Recipes area!
- Check out the Daily Love Dose to get romantic ideas and suggestions.

Visit us online at

www.eHarlequin.com
on Women.com Networks